# Dungeon Games

## A Masters and Mercenaries Novella
## By Lexi Blake

# 1001 Dark Nights

## EVIL EYE
CONCEPTS

Dungeon Games
A Masters and Mercenaries Novella
By Lexi Blake

1001 Dark Nights

Copyright 2014 DLZ Entertainment, LLC
ISBN: 978-1-940887-15-9

Forward: Copyright 2014 M. J. Rose

Published by Evil Eye Concepts, Incorporated

Sign up for the 1001 Dark Nights Newsletter
and be entered to win a Tiffany Key necklace.
There's a contest every month!

Visit www.1001DarkNights.com/key/to subscribe.

As a bonus, all subscribers will receive a free
1001 Dark Nights story on 1/1/15.
*The First Night*
by Shayla Black, Lexi Blake & M.J. Rose

# One Thousand and One Dark Nights

*Once upon a time, in the future…*

*I was a student fascinated with stories and learning.
I studied philosophy, poetry, history, the occult, and
the art and science of love and magic. I had a vast
library at my father's home and collected thousands
of volumes of fantastic tales.*

*I learned all about ancient races and bygone
times. About myths and legends and dreams of all
people through the millennium. And the more I read
the stronger my imagination grew until I discovered
that I was able to travel into the stories... to actually
become part of them.*

*I wish I could say that I listened to my teacher
and respected my gift, as I ought to have. If I had, I
would not be telling you this tale now.
But I was foolhardy and confused, showing off
with bravery.*

*One afternoon, curious about the myth of the
Arabian Nights, I traveled back to ancient Persia to
see for myself if it was true that every day Shahryar
(Persian: شهریار, "king") married a new virgin, and then
sent yesterday's wife to be beheaded. It was written
and I had read, that by the time he met Scheherazade,
the vizier's daughter, he'd killed one thousand
women.*

*Something went wrong with my efforts. I arrived
in the midst of the story and somehow exchanged
places with Scheherazade — a phenomena that had
never occurred before and that still to this day, I
cannot explain.*

*Now I am trapped in that ancient past. I have
taken on Scheherazade's life and the only way I can
protect myself and stay alive is to do what she did to
protect herself and stay alive.*

*Every night the King calls for me and listens as I spin tales.
And when the evening ends and dawn breaks, I stop at a
point that leaves him breathless and yearning for more.
And so the King spares my life for one more day, so that
he might hear the rest of my dark tale.*

*As soon as I finish a story... I begin a new
one... like the one that you, dear reader, have before
you now.*

# Chapter One

Derek Brighton watched the Texas Ranger running the meeting. Clayton Hill was a big guy dressed in pressed jeans and a perfectly ironed western shirt with pearl snaps. Polished boots covered his feet. That dude didn't have to wear craptastic polyester uniforms, and he was pretty sure he didn't have civilians regularly cursing him. He stood tall in the small conference room in the DPD building. Two other members of the Rangers stood in the back. Derek was the only officer representing the Dallas Police Department. It made him nervous that there was so much attention settled straight on him.

The slide changed, throwing ghastly images on the screen.

"The unsub has killed four women we know of," Hill explained. "We're fairly certain his actual number is more. He's smart and clean, so he's likely got several not so clean kills to his credit, and he's smart enough to not get his prints on a vic. We believe he's using latex gloves and has a working knowledge of forensics."

The blond guy in the back snorted a little. He wasn't dressed in typical western wear. He wore a full suit and kept his hair in a far too metro style to actually be a field Ranger. He seemed to be some sort of tech, but both Rangers turned and gave him chilly looks.

"Harris? Do you have something to add?" Hill asked.

The man named Harris held up his hands. "Just saying the dude ain't as smart as me or he wouldn't have pulled the rice trick. Idiot."

Hill turned back. "Ignore him. He's our forensic expert. He's got a genius level IQ and the personality of a jackass. Now back to our unsub. The feds are staying out of it—for now. Let's hope we can solve this before we have to deal with them. The minute they step in, we're all screwed. So all the victims were left in a similar fashion..."

Hill kept talking, but Derek looked at the slide in front of him. A brunette had her hands together, tied in a knot he recognized. Asanawa. *Shit.* There was a reason Hill had chosen him and it wasn't for his location. Three of the killings had occurred outside of his precinct.

*Fuck all.* He'd been outed. After ten years of keeping his proclivities private, someone had talked.

Derek sighed and sat back in his chair. If he was going to get fired, he wouldn't be sitting in on this meeting. He would be in the chief's office getting his ass handed to him. The chief wouldn't care personally. Hell, the chief was a member at Sanctum, but if there was a scandal brewing, he'd have no choice but to throw Derek under the proverbial bus. He was sure they would find some tiny infraction he'd committed. Internal Affairs loved to fire people for taking pencils or using the Internet for personal reasons. Everyone did it, but IA used it as an excuse to get rid of problem officers all the time.

"Do you recognize the rope pattern, Lieutenant?" Clayton Hill's partner had identified himself as Tyler Watts. He was only slightly smaller than his partner, his hair an almost reddish brown. He kept it the tiniest bit longer than Hill and there was at least ten years separating him from the older officer. A Ranger baby. Which meant he was deadlier than the rest, more competent than his age would suggest.

This was the moment. He could shrug and ask why he'd been pulled in here. He could deny everything and maybe, just maybe save his ass in the long run.

The vision of the girl, forever silenced, would haunt him if he didn't speak up. Unfortunately, he hadn't become a cop to save his ass. He'd become a soldier first and then a cop because the need to protect was his highest imperative. He sighed and followed his instincts. He couldn't be less than who he was, wouldn't allow himself to hide when it meant someone's justice might go undone. "Yes. They form a pattern used by practitioners of Japanese rope bondage. Do you have close-ups of the ligature marks?"

Normally he would call them rope marks—a loving reminder of a good time between a sub and Dom, but this wasn't BDSM. BDSM was consensual. Always. He'd heard the term consensual BDSM. Whoever came up with it was a fuck wit. Non-consensual BDSM was assault, battery, rape. It was a crime and should be treated as such.

Harris stepped up, a folder in his hand. "Absolutely. The minute I realized what was happening, I paid close attention to the patterns." He shrugged a little. "I have a girlfriend who read all that *Fifty Shades* stuff. Can't stand it myself, but damn it gets the ladies hawt, if you know what I mean. I've gotten more trim from that damn book. I could kiss EL James. Or hey, I could do her, too."

Harris was annoying as fuck. Derek simply stared at the idiot until he passed him the folder.

"You thought about applying for the Rangers, Brighton?" Watts asked, a smile on his face. "Because you have the intimidating look down."

He flipped the folder open and was assaulted by a look book of horrors. Harris might be an ass, but he understood how to document a crime. He'd taken his time, making a panorama of the victim's torture. Every knot was documented and then removed to show how the rope had burned into the victim's skin, forming patterns.

"He knows what he's doing." Derek had practiced Shibari for years and studied with a Master. This guy knew what he was doing with ropes and knots, but he was brutal. "He understands the lifestyle, but I would say he's not a true believer. He plays at it. He's good with knots, but he's a Master in the narrowest sense of the word."

"What the hell does that mean?" Hill asked, his brows in a confused *V*.

Derek tried not to get his back up. He had to be patient with people who didn't understand the lifestyle. "It means a true Master does what's right for his submissive. This man is a monster who understands the discipline but ignores the philosophy."

Harris grinned. "Told you I was right to bring him in."

Hill rolled his eyes.

The door opened and a bright light blocked the silhouette of a man coming through the doorway. A large man. And then another. Two big-ass dudes were entering what had previously been a nearly empty conference room.

"Is this the right place?" The first shadow asked, though with that accent of his, it came out more like *Is dis ta right place?*

Liam O'Donnell. He would know that accent anywhere. Well, at least he wasn't the only one who'd been outed as a perv, though O'Donnell worked in the private sector.

Hill made a gesture and the lights suddenly came up. Derek could see the second man. Sean Taggart. Tall, blond, built like a linebacker. It was odd that the six foot three inch former Green Beret's nickname was Little Tag, but then his older brother dwarfed him. Ian Taggart had been Derek's commanding officer when he'd been in the Green Berets as well. He knew Big Tag better but was well acquainted with the younger Taggart. Before he'd gotten married and become a chef, Little Tag had worked with his brother at McKay-Taggart, an elite security firm that handled work for corporations, private citizens and—if rumors were true—often did work for the CIA.

Yeah, there was a reason Derek had joined the Dallas Police Department. He'd had enough of the Agency to last a lifetime. He had the scars and the nightmares to prove it. Just thinking about the CIA made a place in his gut ache—the same place where the Taliban had shoved their knives.

"You're in the right place, Mr. O'Donnell, Mr. Taggart." Hill offered them seats, his eyes going back to the door. "Are you alone? I extended the invitation to the rest of your team."

Sean Taggart huffed a little. "Yes, it was such a lovely invite. You know invitations don't usually come with armed escorts. Alex and Eve are on their way in. They were just a bit behind us."

Hill's serious stare told Derek he didn't appreciate the sarcasm. If he was going to work with McKay-Taggart, he'd better get used to it. Sarcasm was their first language.

O'Donnell sank down into the seat next to him, a frown on his face. "Is this your doing, Brighton? You know I just had a kid. I had to leave Avery and Aidan behind with the Paxon sisters because apparently you can't do your job properly."

"Give the guy a break," Little Tag interjected. "You don't understand how law enforcement works in Texas. When the Rangers call, you answer."

"I thought the bloody Rangers were a bad baseball team," O'Donnell grumbled.

And that was all he needed from the Irishman. "Bite my balls, asshole. Don't talk about either Rangers that way." He wouldn't have anybody insult his team on his home turf. God only knew what the Irishman considered real sports. Probably soccer. "I'm not behind this. I got the same invitation, though the Ranger just came to my desk and hauled me in here."

Hill took a step forward, moving with the ease of a predator. "I only sent out the escort because I've heard Taggart can be a jerk."

Watts held out a hand. He was obviously the one who tried to smooth the way for his rougher partner. "Difficult. We'd just heard he could be difficult."

Harris obviously had no worries. He just grinned. "Oh, I've heard he's an enormous ass. I was totally looking forward to meeting him."

Sean snorted a little. "You have no idea. Unfortunately, you picked a shitty time to decide to need his services. My brother is on assignment in England along with half our crew. I'm sitting in for him for a couple of weeks because we're short staffed. Li here just had a kid and so did Adam and Jake. Jake pulled the short straw and had to go across the pond with the rest of them. Adam hid in the bathroom when the asshole escort showed up. I'm getting his ass back for that later. If you were trying to get to big brother, you're going to have to call Tennessee Smith, and good fucking luck with that, man."

Tennessee Smith hadn't been Derek's handler when he'd done the Agency's dirty work, but he knew the man well enough. Even if Hill could find a number for the CIA agent, there was zero chance that Smith would take the call if he was working overseas.

Hill shook his head. "I'd love to have the big guy, but I'll settle for what I have. Consider yourself subject experts. Captain, thanks for joining us."

Shit. Derek's boss walked in and took a seat. Great. He needed his boss to hear this. The captain simply nodded his way and gave him a quick hello.

The Ranger turned to the door again. "Ah, and there's the one I really wanted to see. Hello, darlin'."

"Hello, Clayton," a smooth feminine voice said. There was a warm welcome in her tone. "It's nice to see you again."

Derek turned to see Eve McKay stride into the room. She was a former profiler for the FBI and it looked like she'd done some work for the Rangers as well if her warm greeting for Hill was any indication. She was dressed in a chic business suit, her blonde hair pulled back in a business-like bun. She was followed by her hulking beast of a husband who also served as her Dom. She stopped and allowed him to move in front of her, their ease with each other obvious to everyone in the room.

Eve allowed her husband to go first, allowed him to find a seat for her, allowed him to assess any threats in the room before following him. Eve was a submissive and a proper one at that. She was lovely and controlled and trusted her Dom with her safety and comfort and life.

So unlike Karina. Karina was always the slightest bit messy when she wasn't in fet wear. She typically wore her hair in a ponytail, the pure raven strands flying out at odd angles. She often didn't wear makeup and outside the club wouldn't wear a damn thing on her feet besides those nasty looking sneakers she claimed were comfortable. Eve was the gracious submissive and Karina was a self-described tough chick.

He didn't do tough chicks. Even when he really fucking wanted to. Even when they called to him. Even when his dick jumped at the sound of her voice.

Nope. He'd done the modern relationship thing. He wouldn't go there again. It ended in frustration and divorce. He didn't need another "modern" woman to emasculate him. His wife had done the job quite well.

His ex. Fuck all. Just like that he knew why he was here. "Maia. Maia told you."

Maia Brighton—because god knew she couldn't be bothered to change her name after the divorce—was one of the Dallas District Attorney's Office's hottest lawyers. In more ways than one. She was damn fine at her job and from what Derek could tell, she'd also slept with most of her bosses. And she was just the type to give up his kinks and those of his friends if she thought it would take her an extra step up the ladder.

Hill nodded shortly. "Harris came up with the idea of bringing in subject experts on this case, Detective. I asked the DA's office if they knew of any and they were happy to oblige."

Derek's boss, Captain Joe Harrigan, leaned forward in his seat. "Derek, the Rangers here have promised to be discreet. As far as anyone knows, you're going to be working this case because you've worked more homicides than anyone else in the division."

"I'm not going to get my ass kicked for my private life?" He wouldn't be the first cop to find himself shoved off the force for not toeing the very narrow line.

Joe snorted a little, as did Alex McKay as he slid into his seat after settling Eve into hers. "You're not the only one with kinks, man," the captain said. "The chief belongs to a club himself."

Derek relaxed a little. If the chief had said something to his captain, then everything was cool. He was a good cop. He'd always done his best and had been told he was in line for promotions. Maybe the department wasn't so rigid. "So you're looking for BDSM experts because you think the killer is prowling BDSM clubs?"

"All of the women he's killed have been known submissives in the community. Including the latest." Hill's whole face went grave and he glanced at Joe, who nodded. There was a heavy tension permeating the air.

*Oh, fuck.* They were holding back on him. He looked between the two men, searching their faces as they held a silent conversation between them that ended with Joe sighing heavily and placing his hand on the folder he'd brought in.

Derek's stomach took a nose dive.

"Who?" There was only one reason for him to touch that folder like he didn't want to release it, like there was something sacred in it and the information would change things.

"He killed again, early this morning. It's why we brought you in so suddenly," Joe explained.

*Fuck. Fuck. Fuck.* He stared at the folder like it was a snake that would bite him if he moved even an inch. Very slowly, as though time had turned into a mud pit he had to slog through, Joe slid that folder his way.

"I'm sorry to have to tell you this way, Brighton. The latest victim is someone you know," Hill explained, his deep voice grim. "It's someone you all know. Apparently she was a regular at that club your brother owns, Sean. Sanctum?"

Sean had gone a little white, his eyes on the folder, too. "Yes."

"Oh, my god." Eve reached for her husband, tears already in her eyes.

"Fuck me," O'Donnell said, running a hand through his hair. "It's not Jill or Ashley. I just left them."

All around him they were chattering, but it seemed to come from a distance because his hand was on that folder and his stomach was somewhere in his throat. He was a cop who'd seen the absolute worst things humanity could do both in war and in the civilian sector. He could handle just about anything, but he was going to make a fool of himself if he turned that folder over and saw her in a photograph, her gorgeous blue eyes dead and that skin of hers cold.

*Not Karina. Not Karina. Not Karina.*

He suddenly wondered who it would be okay to see in that picture and he realized a brutal and nasty truth. Anyone but her. He could handle it being anyone except her. He was friends with the subs at Sanctum. He'd slept with some of them, and he suddenly knew he would toss them all to the wolves if it meant Karina was still breathing. It was perverse because he wasn't even friends with her. He was never going to be close to her, but he couldn't stand the thought of never seeing her again.

*Not Karina. Not Karina. Not Karina.*

He turned over the folder and a golden-haired blonde with blue eyes was staring up at him. He'd seen those blue eyes before, but now there was nothing lighting them. They were flat and empty in death.

"Holy shite," O'Donnell breathed as he looked over Derek's shoulder. "I didn't like the girl, but damn me if I want that to happen to anyone."

Amanda. Guilt swamped in and yet he couldn't help but feel a massive wave of relief. *Not Karina. Amanda.* She'd been a junior officer, a first-class bitch, and he'd had a hand in ousting her from Sanctum. Now she was dead, a victim. She was a cop and all he could think about was Karina. He was a pathetic waste. He should feel more for a woman he'd worked with. He'd topped Amanda on many occasions, but deep down it had just been an exchange of need. There hadn't been a single emotion for her beyond anger when she'd threatened to bring down the club.

Shouldn't it mean more?

"Officer King was found dead in an alley behind a club in Deep Ellum early this morning," Joe said in a monotone that let Derek know he was in full-on cop mode. Nothing would touch him until he'd gotten the job done.

That cold professionalism was nothing less than what he owed to his fallen officer.

Derek adopted the same and tried his damnedest to not feel the relief in his gut that Karina was still walking the earth in her atrocious shoes.

Because it didn't matter. She wasn't his type and she was kind of a righteous bitch who had it in for him, which was why he wished she would stop looking at him with her doe eyes and stop walking around the club with her big, gorgeous tits hanging out, and wished she would disappear so he could fucking sleep with someone else because he damn straight wasn't going to sleep with her.

No way. No fucking how.

Professional. He had to stay cool and calm because there was a killer working and he'd come straight into Derek's world.

"Amanda was no longer a member of Sanctum. We have very strict rules on how submissives enter and leave the club. She would never have been allowed to walk to her vehicle alone. She would have been walked to her car and she would have been asked to call another member of the club when she got safely home. If she hadn't made the call, someone would have gone looking for her," Alex McKay explained as Derek ran through the details that made up the end of Amanda's life.

Strangled with jute rope. He stared at the pictures, recognizing the tortoise-shaped pattern of ropes that crossed her naked flesh. A rope dress. The bastard had used an intricate pattern to truss her up.

"Yes, we think she was in one of the larger clubs, a not so private one. There are two we've identified in the DFW area and that's where we need your help," Hill explained.

"You want us to go undercover," Sean surmised.

"Eve isn't going anywhere," McKay said immediately. "She can profile the fucker for you, but if he's killing subs, you can't expect me to send her in."

Watts stepped up. "Look, we don't need a sub. We've got a good line on a sub to send in. I haven't talked to her myself, but we've identified her as a potential victim. We found her name on a grain of rice the unsub left on Officer King."

"We?" Harris said, his eyes wide.

Clayton pointed a finger Harris's way. "Just explain the findings. We don't need a ton of attitude."

Harris straightened his tie and smirked for all he was worth. "They didn't even realize it was there. I didn't work the first couple of cases. The other guy is an idiot. I found it this morning. It was very small, a little trace. He's looking to lead us down a rabbit hole and no one had found the way yet."

Oh, Derek was so glad he didn't have to work with this asshole on a regular basis. "Are you going to explain or just give us a lot of literary references?"

"But they're good references. You have to admit I have style." He sighed a little. "Fine. Besides the obvious bondage, I found something odd in her hair. I've got a very specific routine. I check every inch of the victim. I don't miss a damn thing. I found something weird in her hair. A grain of rice. A lesser tech would have missed it or thought it was a coincidence. Maybe she'd been cooking earlier. But it didn't get past me. That was a clue and I had a feeling about it."

Hill huffed a little. "I want to murder him myself half the time, but he's got uncanny instincts."

"What does rice have to do with this?" Liam asked.

Harris rubbed his hands together in obvious delight. "So much. It's the little things that truly make a crime a work of art. I bagged that grain of rice and it was the first thing I studied. I knew it was meaningful. I got it under my scope and that was when I found it. A name was written right fucking there. We've gone back through the other victims and in each case there was a single grain of rice with the next victim's name on it. Who the flying fuck does that?"

Alex frowned. "How the hell did he get it on there?"

It was the kind of thing he'd seen at amusement parks and festivals. *Your Name on a Grain of Rice.* He'd seen booths offering the keepsake a couple of times. He'd never heard of it being left on a victim.

"You know the name of the submissive you think is going to be the unsub's next victim?" Eve asked. "I would love to talk to her. I know a bit about Amanda. If you would give me information on the other victims and let me talk to this woman, it would help me with a profile. I assume that's why I'm here."

Hill nodded. "I need you, Eve. You've done amazing work for us in the past. I've been given the go-ahead to pay your usual rate and double if you have to work overtime."

She shook her head. "No. This is pro bono, Clay."

Alex agreed. "McKay-Taggart is at your service. This is personal. Just tell us what you need."

"I think he needs one of us to act as the next victim's Dom," Sean said.

Hill nodded. "We need one of you to make contact with the potential victim. We're bringing her in to talk, but we thought a friendly face might help to sway her to work with us. She should be here in a few hours. I'm going to brief you and then you can help explain it all to her. We need her. If she decides to run, we might lose him and he'll kill another girl."

A cold feeling hit his stomach. He'd always had an uncanny sense of when the shit was about to hit the fan, and it threatened to take him over now. Someone he knew?

"What's her name?" The question was tight, forced from his throat.

"Karina. Karina Mills. She's a private detective from what I understand. I was told you know her quite well. It's why I actually think we might have caught a break. She should be good undercover, right?"

She wasn't working undercover. They wanted bait. Pretty, sweet bait with spectacular tits and an ass he'd been dying to spank.

"I'll do it. I'll be her Dom." He was startled to hear the words coming out of his mouth, but he wouldn't take them back.

"Damn straight you will," Alex said. "You're the only one of us who can, Derek. Simon and Jesse are in England. Tag will kick our asses if Karina gets murdered. She's practically on the payroll."

One of us. That was what McKay was talking about. Amanda might have gone to Sanctum, but Karina was truly one of them. Karina was a fixture at both Sanctum and McKay-Taggart. She was also a pain in his ass.

*And this is your shot to get your hands on her, dickhead. Don't fucking blow it. You'll have to be with her, sleep close to her, protect her. You can fuck her and get her out of your system and then you won't have this ache in your gut every time she walks in a room. You can be free of her. You'll see it wouldn't ever work. You'll know.*

"I'll take care of her. This is my case." He needed to use the words his old Army buddies would recognize and respect. "My op."

His op. His way. His charge.

*Fuck.* Karina Mills was going to be in his care, his responsibility.

One way or another, he would save her. Whether she liked it or not.

\* \* \* \*

Karina Mills looked out the window of the conference room and wondered exactly what the hell she'd done to piss the DPD off. She had to admit, it was the first time in a long time she'd had her ass hauled to jail.

*Hey, Kevin, at least this time I wasn't in cuffs.*

It was so hard to stand in a police department and not think of him. Years had passed and she could still remember how he looked sitting at his desk in Brooklyn, the one across from his partner. It was always neat as a pin, perfectly organized. Perfect. Like Kevin himself. Her smiling protector.

Unlike that asshole Derek Brighton, who always frowned her way. Always made her feel like she was dirt underneath his shoe. The one and only time they'd played together had been beyond awkward because they'd been in the middle of a case that ended with him accusing her of impeding an investigation and her siccing IA on his ass in revenge.

She shouldn't have done it, but she wasn't sure how to apologize.

And it was likely for the best because they didn't fit.

So why was she so damn attracted to him? Why did she sit around and wonder why he smiled at all the other subs but never had one for her? Why did he and he alone have the capacity to make her remember who she really was?

She could clean herself up. She could do good. She could fly right, but underneath all of it, she was still a junkie.

Once an addict, always an addict. She was one misstep away from sticking a needle in her arm, and the minute she forgot it, she would fall off the very sturdy wagon she'd built for herself.

Thank god for sealed records or she wouldn't have a job at all. She seriously doubted McKay-Taggart would pay her intensely high fees if Big Tag knew she'd been a high school drug addict and minor criminal. Li O'Donnell likely wouldn't play cards with her, and he certainly wouldn't let her anywhere near his precious Avery.

She would lose all her friends. Ashley and Jill would probably back away. It was just what people did when they realized how badly she'd fucked up in the past.

Need rose, hard and fast. The need to get out of herself for a while, to not think about anything, to shut her never-ending thoughts up. She very calmly took a long drink of coffee. Bitter. Not a hint of sweet. Just like she liked it. She stared out and thought about hitting a meeting. She would find the nearest one the minute she got out of here.

Hiding who she was—it was a no no in the book of sobriety and yet she couldn't make herself talk about it to her new friends. Couldn't put herself out there to be judged and found wanting.

She didn't even want to think about what Lieutenant Brighton would do if he found out about her past. He would likely give her his trademark hot-guy smirk and tell her he'd always known there was something wrong with her.

Or worse, he would look at her with pity.

She took a deep breath and for the millionth time wished Kevin hadn't died. Wished he'd been less of a hero. Wished her Dom, her husband, was still with her, easing her way through life, teaching her control and the beauty of submission and trust.

*If anything ever happens to me, you be brave, Karina. You be the woman I know you can be. You don't have to accept who you were. Be the you you want to be. My beautiful wife. My strong sub.*

Guilt gnawed at her gut because as much as she'd loved Kevin

Mills, she'd never felt the shock of lust she got the minute Derek Brighton walked into a room. It was perverse. It was wrong.

Sometimes it was all she thought about. Years and years had gone by without sex and she was all right with it for the most part. Only Derek had sparked the need in her.

The door opened and Karina turned, frowning as a whole line of people she knew very well walked in.

Eve and Alex McKay were followed by Sean Taggart and Liam O'Donnell, and that gorgeous bastard Brighton. She looked at him freely because he so rarely glanced her way. She was free to study him since he avoided her eyes. He was roughly six two with a pelt of brown and gold hair he kept in a cut that would have made his old CO proud. There was just the hint of a five o'clock shadow on his jaw, though it was barely one o'clock in the afternoon. He probably shaved twice a day, as though his masculinity was always trying to make itself known. She'd thought often about kissing that rigid jawline of his until it softened.

Not that he would ever soften for her.

She could stare at him for hours and it was all right because he avoided her.

Except this time his eyes came up. Brown eyes that always seemed so cold now heated as he stopped and stared at her, his eyes going from hers to her breasts and hips in a bold assessment and then right back to lock stares with her.

A challenge. She felt a little huff of breath leave her and then she averted her eyes out of habit. He was staring at her the way a Dom would when sizing up a sub, and she'd been trained on how to act. She caught the hint of a smirk hit his face and then turned from him.

She didn't have to take that from him. He wasn't her Dom and he never would be.

"Hey, guys. What's up?" She asked the question casually, but suspicion was creeping into her brain. Why had she been brought to the police station if Big Tag wanted a meeting? He typically just called her private cell and told her to get her ass to a place of his choosing and then he bitched that she overcharged him and asked when she was going to implement a coupon program.

Would he send in Alex McKay to let her know he wouldn't do business with her anymore? Tag always seemed like a man who would do his own dirty work.

Eve walked straight up to her and threw her arms around her, hugging her tight.

Karina understood the value of a hug. She immediately opened her arms, not questioning her friend. Eve was tense, her whole body shaking slightly. Karina's heart opened. She put a soothing hand in Eve's perfect hair. "It's all right, honey." Eve was good people. "Whatever happened, I'll help you. I promise."

Alex came up, his green eyes kind. "Amanda King was murdered last night."

Karina was the one holding on to Eve now. Amanda had been a sub at Sanctum. She'd been the troublesome one, attempting to be a Queen Bee. She'd had a hard outer shell Karina had never been able to crack, but that didn't mean she didn't feel the loss. She'd known the woman.

"You could have been a little gentler, Alex," Derek complained.

But Karina knew there was no gentle way to deal with death. And she had a sudden suspicion of why she'd really been called in. How did he know? How the hell had the detective figured out she was working a case that involved a dead sub? Tanya Wilson's mother had begged her to find her baby girl. Unfortunately, Karina had found the police report that led her to Jane Doe, who turned out to be Tanya. Sweet kid. Twenty-fucking-two years old. She'd been beaten and raped and her body had been dumped in an alley like she didn't matter. Like she'd never mattered. Like she hadn't hugged her momma before she went to sleep and led her high school debate team to a regional championship. Her life had been taken and pared down to nothing.

And Karina couldn't accept that. Tanya Wilson's great crime seemed to have been experimenting sexually in the D/s arts. A monster had lured her in and then made perverse something that should have been sacred. Karina had a five hundred dollar retainer with the promise of absolutely nothing else and she was on the case. She would find whoever had left Tanya Wilson's mother in perpetual mourning for the child she'd lost.

She'd been very quiet about it, not wanting to tip anyone off. It had occurred to her to ask Simon Weston to work with her, but he'd been called away to London on another case and she'd lost her shot. She couldn't ask the others. They were all married and she loved their wives. She couldn't pull the husbands away. And she sure as hell wouldn't ask the lieutenant. He would just as likely toss her ass in jail as work with her.

Was he going to do that now?

A man she'd never met before walked into the room, and Karina's eyes widened. Stetson hat. Pressed blue jeans. Bolo tie over a dress shirt.

*Damn.* The Rangers were involved. If they were involved, it meant she'd been on the right track all along.

"It's a serial case. Shit." She flushed a little, stepping to Eve's side. "I'm sorry to have cursed, sir."

Derek Brighton's eyes flared. "You've never been sorry before."

Had he thought she was talking to him? She hadn't meant Sir, but rather had simply meant to be polite to the baddest ass in the room. If there was one thing she'd learned since she'd moved to Texas, it was to respect the highest authority in law enforcement. "I was talking to the Ranger."

The big guy tipped his head her way. He was a glorious specimen of masculinity. She put his age at forty and it looked good on him. "Ma'am. I'm Clayton Hill with the Texas Rangers. It's a pleasure to meet you, Miss Mills. I'm sorry it's under such tragic circumstances. You knew the victim?"

She hated the fact that Amanda was being referred to as the victim, but she understood the need to distance. She knew what it meant to be a cop's wife. They dealt with the worst things a human could see. They had to have distance to do their jobs and maintain some sanity. "Yes."

His blue eyes held a wealth of sympathy and he reached out for her hand, grasping it between his. "Then I'm especially sorry for your loss."

Derek was right there, grasping her elbow and pulling her away from the lovely Ranger. "We need to move on. We have very little time. According to everything we know about this guy, he'll strike again in the next two weeks."

Her head was whirling a bit as Derek hauled her toward the conference table and pulled out a chair for her. If she'd had a minute to think about it, she would have found another chair out of sheer stubbornness, but he moved so fast, she found herself settled in next to him in an instant. "We know something about this guy?"

She didn't even know there was a guy on their radar. The last time she'd talked to the local police, they were checking out Tanya's ex-boyfriend as the main suspect. She seriously doubted the college kid had been running around killing subs.

Derek frowned her way, but then that was his usual expression when it came to her. "Why did you ask if this was a serial case? Do you know something?"

She bit her bottom lip, a nervous habit. So they didn't know? "I'm kind of working a case."

His frown deepened. "A case? What kind of a case?"

"I started working a missing persons case a few weeks ago. The girl was playing in some clubs. Tanya Wilson. My missing person became a murder investigation."

There it went again. If he frowned any more, she was pretty sure his face would turn in on itself. "The second victim?"

She felt her eyes widen. She'd known there was more to this. It just felt wrong to her. "How many vics have we got so far?"

*Holy shit.* She'd been hunting a serial. She'd had that feeling in the pit of her gut. It was why she hadn't been to Sanctum for weeks. She'd been busy letting herself be seen at the more dangerous clubs, the ones Tanya had frequented.

Alex sat down in front of her, Eve sliding in on his side. "Four that we've found. Karina, there's something you should know."

"What?" Yes, something was so wrong because Alex put a hand over hers as though giving her comfort for the horror to come.

"The Rangers identified the woman he's targeting as his next victim."

A little thrill ran through her and now she let herself grin. Oh, she was good. Damn good. Now that she knew what was going on, there was really only one reason to bring her in. Only one reason Alex looked scared to give her the news.

He had no idea she'd been trying to make this happen for weeks.

"It's you, Karina," Derek said with a grim finality.

"Fuck, yeah!" She got out of her chair and did a little fist pump. "Finally something goes right."

She couldn't help but notice Derek had turned the brightest shade of red.

Well, she couldn't win them all.

# Chapter Two

Derek herded her into his office. Herded? Hell, he'd practically picked her hot ass up and run away with her after the hour-long briefing because all he could think about was wiping that self-satisfied smile off her face. From the moment she'd fist pumped like a teenager winning a video game, he'd thought of nothing but getting her alone.

Karina Mills thought it was awesome that she'd managed to get a serial killer to notice her? Well, she was going to get some serious attention from her brand new Dom, and there was no way she was going to like it.

She turned on her heels, a frown on that gorgeous face of hers. "All right, Detective. You've got me alone. You want to tell me what crawled up your ass and died a slow and obviously painful death?"

He was going to enjoy the next few moments because it *was* painfully obvious to him that she hadn't understood a damn thing about the way this was going to work. Clayton Hill had used technical words like "liaise" and "report to." Derek was about to use a few words Karina would fully recognize and then he'd see if she was still ready to jump up and down with excitement.

He ignored her very rude question as he walked around his office, shutting the blinds with a careful hand. Privacy was required for what he was about to do. He could hear her foot begin to tap against the floor.

She was such an impatient woman. They would have to work on that.

He took a minute to gather himself, to calm down. They had to work together. This was a serious case. Alex and Eve McKay were still closed up with the Rangers and their forensic expert, going over all the technical details that would help Eve profile their killer. Sean and Liam were on their way to Karina's apartment to set up additional security, including cameras. They were going to take jobs at one of the clubs Karina had been frequenting.

Alone. She'd been visiting clubs without even bothering to tell anyone where she was. The clubs weren't known for their safety. Derek would never take a sub there and yet Karina had walked right in without any backup.

Fuck, he was getting pissed again. And his cock was hard as a damn rock.

"Are you having trouble, Brighton? Should I get someone? Because I need to go and meet Little Tag and Li. We've got a bunch of stuff to go over before tonight's op." She talked like she was doing an everyday job. Nothing to be concerned about. She wasn't throwing herself in front of a known serial killer or anything.

"We'll talk to Sean and Li when I'm through discussing the situation with you." He had to get his unruly dick under control.

"Well, I'm done now, Brighton. I'll send you a report." She sighed a little. "I don't know why I can't just work through the Rangers. I get that DPD wants to protect its turf. I really do understand that. How about we work something out? I promise to keep you in the loop. I'll talk to you on a daily basis and keep you up to date. If your chief asks, you're totally in on this. But you certainly don't have to watch over me."

She had a bad habit of hearing what she wanted to hear. He had to correct that behavior, too. For the first time in a very long time, he found his blood pulsing at the thought. The last several years, the training he'd given to various submissives had been delivered with a practiced hand. It had been something he looked forward to, something that made him feel needed.

Discipline had been something he enjoyed delivering, but now his blood was pumping through his system and he realized exactly what he'd been missing. He'd deeply missed the game, the thrill that came from taming a sub to his hand.

This sub. Unruly. Arrogant. Gorgeous. Could he turn her into a sweet little kitten?

It was a bad idea and yet the thought of even playing with her got his dick stiff and aching. It wasn't like she was looking for a permanent Dom. She liked to play at Sanctum. She wasn't really submissive. She was the type of woman who played at it for sex. As far as he could tell, Karina had slept with several of the Doms, the latest being Simon Weston. She'd hooked up with O'Donnell and Big Tag before they'd gotten married. Maybe after, too. Her relationships were fairly shallow and she didn't seem to require much more from her men than a good time in bed and a deft hand with a flogger. He could give her both.

Would it really be so bad to take what she had to offer?

"Brighton?" Annoyance was creeping into her voice. "I don't have all day. What do you say? We pretend to work together?"

"I'm not going to pretend, Karina. We are going to be working together."

He heard her sigh. "That's a bad idea. Can't you see that?"

"Why?" He'd love to know why she couldn't seem to stand him.

"Because you don't like me."

He heard a wealth of possibilities in those words. For the first time since he'd met her, he heard some vulnerability. "That's funny. I thought you were the one who didn't like me."

"Derek, you can't stand me."

He owed her some honesty. He gave it to her in the plainest fashion he could. He turned around and let her see the state of his cock. "Oh, there are parts of me that like you quite a bit, Karina."

He couldn't help but smile at the way her eyes widened, her mouth dropping open. Finally, finally he'd managed to shut her up and all he'd had to do was point a dick her way. If he'd known it would be that easy, he would have tried it a long time back. After all, he was always hard when she was around anyway.

He moved toward his desk with care. Now that he had her attention, it was time to talk to her. "Why don't you have a seat, Karina?"

She shook her head, nibbling on that plump bottom lip of hers. "This is a bad idea."

"You've said that several times. It's not an idea. It's what's going to happen." He sat down, happy to have some furniture between them. He gestured to the seat in front of him. "We seem to have been in two different meetings. You're not in charge of this operation, Karina."

She finally moved to the chair, her body folding as she sank down. Maia had been perfectly graceful, every move and action of her body a dance of seduction. Karina just plopped down and slumped over slightly.

Why was he so fucking fascinated with her? Why this woman? He appreciated grace and precision, but he couldn't deny that Karina Mills fucked with his system. She looked so lost, he had the sudden impulse to pull her into his lap and have the whole conversation with his hand teasing her pussy, relaxing her.

Of course she wasn't wearing a handy, frothy skirt. No. None of that for tough PI Karina. She had on a sturdy pair of jeans and a high-necked T-shirt. Masculine. He preferred her in a corset and thong.

"The Rangers are in charge, Brighton."

As attempts to regain control went, Derek thought it was fairly weak. "Yes, the Rangers are in charge of the investigation, but I'm in charge of you."

Let her sit on that for a moment.

"No."

"Yes." It was time to get a little firm. "You will report to me during this operation or I'll have you in protective custody and in a safe house before you can take your next breath. If, at any time, I decide you're a danger to the operation or yourself, I'll place you in protective custody. If you step out of line or disobey me, I'll..."

"Have me in protective custody," Karina finished with a bitter note. "Yeah, I get it. I know this case better than you."

She was obviously recovering. "You didn't even realize it was a serial case."

"Yeah, well, you didn't even realize it was a case at all, Mr. Hotshot Homicide Detective. I bet Amanda wishes you hadn't dropped the ball on that one."

There was the righteous bitch he knew so well. She was hard on a man's ego and she'd managed to score a perfect shot. Amanda had given everyone around her hell, but that didn't mean he wanted her dead. He should have protected her, should have seen what was going to happen.

"Derek, I shouldn't have said that." She leaned forward, her eyes sympathetic. "That was rude of me, but it points out all the reasons we shouldn't work together. Believe it or not, I'm actually quite thoughtful. I'm very rarely rude to anyone, but you bring out the worst in me."

And the deep need to lash right back at her had damn near overwhelmed him. Somehow she managed to hurt him more than anyone else. He'd always given in to those instincts before, but he needed to deal with her fairly and in a D/s fashion. "We should settle on punishments first then. Every time you're rude to me, it's a count of twenty. I don't expect you to obey me in everyday life, but when we're working, there will be stiff punishments for any infraction of the rules. I understand that you're a professional investigator, but you are no longer in charge of this case. You will turn over everything you have to the Rangers and consider yourself under my charge until this is cleared up."

He kind of loved the fact that her jaw had dropped and she shook her head in a slightly stunned fashion. "No. I...no."

He reached for the phone. "All right. I'll make sure the protective custody officers find you someplace nice."

It wouldn't be nice. It would be some rathole because that would be all the department could afford. He was sure if Big Tag hadn't been traipsing around Europe he would lean on someone and get Karina off the hook, but without him, Karina was at Derek's mercy.

And he had none. Damn, but it was good to have the advantage for once in his life.

Her hand shot out, staying the call. "Don't. I'm not spending the next two weeks in some fleabag motel eating bad takeout. This is stupid, Derek. You can't want this. Besides, isn't it going to throw this guy off if I suddenly show up with a Dom?"

"Two of the vics had full-time Doms. Amanda had been seen playing with a Dom she'd dated for a month. She hadn't been collared, but he was with her just a few hours before her death. The unsub doesn't give a shit about whether you're taken or not. Very likely he'll find it a challenge to try to kill you right under my nose." Something about the crimes screamed arrogance to Derek. This perp was proud of his work. He was showing off.

"Or he'll get scared off."

"That's better than the alternative."

"What alternative?"

"He actually kills you."

She snorted, an entirely unfeminine sound that he should have found offensive. Should have. "Like I would let that happen."

"Amanda was a cop. She might have had a nasty personality, but don't think for a second that she didn't know how to handle herself. She'd taken all of her self-defense courses. She was perfectly fit. And she's dead. So I don't give a damn what you think you can handle. You can handle working with me or..."

She snarled a little as she finished the sentence for him. "...go into protective custody. You're starting to sound like a broken record, Brighton. You need to get some new material. Damn it. You see what you push me to? I am not this girl."

"Whichever girl you are, she's racking up the punishment." He pushed his chair out a little, giving himself room to work. "I'm going to give you the earlier rude remarks. But it's time to begin as we mean to go, so I'm going to demand payment for the last volley. Twenty over my lap. Let's get this out of the way and then we can get something to eat and talk about this like adults. We need a contract in place. I'd like to go over your hard and soft limits."

He was going to sign a contract with Karina Mills. Earlier it had seemed like the worst idea in the world, and now he couldn't wait to get her signature. It would be proof that she belonged to him for however short a time.

Karina stood, but she wasn't moving toward him. She backed away. "You can't be serious, Brighton. You can't expect that I'll let you spank me right here."

Patience. He needed an enormous amount of patience to deal with her. That was what he'd forgotten during earlier encounters. Karina required patience and a very firm hand. He hadn't been patient with her the one time they'd played before. He'd been awkward. He was going to handle her better this time around. "I don't merely expect it, Karina. I require it. You're going to unzip your pants, push them down, and settle your bare ass over my lap. You're going to allow me to discipline you because that's what Doms and subs do. Are you trying to tell me you don't enjoy a spanking? Or is it just that you think you won't enjoy one from me?"

"I didn't…I didn't think I would get one from you. Ever."

"Ever, Sir," he corrected.

Tears pooled in her eyes. "Are you trying to humiliate me?"

He softened slightly. "I wouldn't do that. I take the lifestyle seriously, and it would please me if you would call me Sir in intimate situations. I'm trying to keep you alive, Karina. And don't you want to know? I know I do."

"What do you want to know?"

"I want to know just how good it's going to feel to fuck you. I want to know if we can take all the energy between us and turn it into something that makes us both feel good for a change. I'm going to be honest with you, Karina. You are not my type. I can't see anything working between us, but god I can't get you out of my head. I can't stop thinking about you, and it's affecting my life."

She stared at him for a minute. Just when he thought she was going to tell him to go to hell, she sighed a little. "I think about you, too. I don't want to. I don't want a relationship with you."

He was a little surprised at how much that hurt. He didn't want a relationship with her either. He meant what he'd said. She wasn't even close to his type. But for some reason she called to him. "I'm going to offer you a deal, Karina. For the duration of this investigation I want to top you. I want to get you out of my system."

"You want to sleep with me?"

"Yes, but I'm not going to require it. I do intend to do my damnedest to seduce you."

"And when the case is done?"

"We try to be friends, maybe? We can at least be friendly. I don't like the friction between us. We see each other too often to keep on the way we have."

Something infinitely sad passed across her face, and he was sure he'd lost her. In that moment, he would have done just about anything to take back the last couple of moments and start over.

She nodded suddenly and crossed the space between them. "Yes, Sir. I think we can make that work."

Her hands went to the button on her jeans and Derek felt his cock jump. He stared as she began to push her pants down and wondered if anything would ever be the same again.

* * * *

What the hell was she doing? She couldn't actually be thinking about shoving her jeans off her hips and offering her ass to Derek Brighton. Because that was insane.

So why were her fingers working the fly of her jeans? Why was she dragging the zipper down and trying to remember what kind of underwear she'd put on this morning. Clean. Yeah, they were clean, but she doubted they were sexy. She tended to wear utilitarian clothes when she was working, a sort of armor that reminded her she had to be tough to do her job.

"Do you need help?" His voice was deep, dark, like rich chocolate. God, just the sound of it made her body light up.

What the hell would she do when he turned that voice on her during play? Likely anything he wanted.

"Give me just a second." She remembered her manners. "Please, Sir."

He nodded.

Why was it so much easier at the club? She had zero problems walking around Sanctum basically naked. She'd long ago accepted that she was an exhibitionist. Being naked felt good. When she was home alone, she rarely wore clothes unless she was cold. God only knew how many spankings she'd taken in her life. She enjoyed it. Another kink she accepted about herself.

Derek had seen her naked. He'd been at Sanctum plenty of times when she'd scened with one of her Dom friends. He'd seen the whole package, so why was she suddenly so self-conscious?

"If it helps, I think you're beautiful, Karina."

Kindness. It was the one thing that almost always disarmed her. She hadn't had a whole lot of kindness from Derek Brighton, but then she hadn't given him much of a chance. From the moment she'd laid eyes on him and felt that white-hot attraction she'd never felt before, she'd put up a wall between them.

"I thought I wasn't your type." She'd hated hearing those words and yet she fully understood that they weren't compatible.

His mouth turned down, showing lines she hadn't noticed before. Worry lines. She wanted to smooth them away. "I can still appreciate how beautiful you are. You know what I want from a submissive, right?"

She'd certainly heard the rumors. "You want a twenty-four seven relationship."

"I do. I want a submissive who trusts me enough to take care of her. I want to be responsible for her. I want to take care of her financially, physically, and emotionally."

She couldn't do that. She knew deep down she wouldn't be happy in that kind of a relationship. She enjoyed D/s, craved it, but she couldn't give him what he needed. And she wasn't sure she wanted to. She'd had the love of her life. A person only got one of those. He'd died five years before and she'd been alone ever since, likely would remain alone for all but small patches of time. She wouldn't marry again, but did that mean she couldn't ever have the comfort of another body against hers? The D/s scenes she performed with her friends didn't ease the ache of loneliness inside her.

Was it really so wrong to take Derek up on his offer? Had she planned to spend the rest of her life without ever taking another lover?

"Just for the case." She heard herself saying the words and her heart fluttered.

"Just for the case," Derek agreed and patted his lap. "Trust me enough to take care of you as a Dom and as your partner."

She was either in or out. It was so obvious. If she walked out the door, they might be able to work together, but she would never know why he made her heart pound in her chest when he walked in a room. Why did it have to be this one man? Why couldn't it have been her husband who had earned her love?

Karina's hands were shaking as she pushed the jeans over her hips and exposed her backside. Crisp chilly air hit her skin, but she still felt hot. Like her skin was too tight and she couldn't make it stretch.

She pushed the jeans and underwear down and turned with as much grace as she could muster. She'd been in the lifestyle for a very long time, so she could handle turning with her legs bound. She managed to place herself over his lap and stared down at the floor.

Time seemed to stop. She stared at the clear plastic that protected the floor where Derek's chair was placed. This was where he sat every day, and now he would have the memory of her laid out over his thighs. And she would have the memory of the way his cock pressed against her belly. He was so hard. Was that for her?

His hand covered her cheek, a soft touch as though he was the one hesitating now.

"Like I said, I think you're quite beautiful, Karina. How long have you been in Dallas?"

His fingertips were skimming her ass, drawing out the anticipation of what would happen. She wanted to squirm, to make him move faster. She kind of thought he wouldn't take that well. She settled for honesty. He had questions? She would give him answers. "Almost four years, Sir."

She'd stayed in their Brooklyn apartment until she couldn't handle the memories a second longer. She'd come to Dallas because she'd worked a job or two for Big Tag, and she didn't have anywhere else to go. The heat of Texas hadn't burned away her memories, but she'd been able to find her balance.

"You lived in New York?"

How little did he know about her? She figured after she'd called IA on his ass a year ago that he would do a search on her. "Yes. I was born in Queens, moved to Brooklyn. I decided I needed a change and Big Tag offered me a job."

She didn't mention Kevin. Somehow the thought of even saying her husband's name seemed wrong here. This was between her and Derek.

His hand stopped its soft progress and he cupped her suddenly. "You're not to make a sound unless it's to tell me to stop. Do you understand?"

Oh, fuck. He was going to do it. He was going to lay that big, callused hand on her backside and light her up. Her whole body went on alert, waiting for that second that he touched her again, for the little uptake of air that would be followed by the sound of his hand cracking on her ass and the flare of pain that signaled that she could rest.

Tears pricked her eyes because it had been so fucking long. So long since she hadn't simply scheduled this, since it came out of nowhere and she could turn her brain off for just a few seconds. She placed her hands on the floor to balance. She didn't know how much he would want her to touch him so she wasn't sure where to place her hands.

"Karina, do you understand?"

"Yes, Sir."

"Do you need this as much as I do?" The question came out on the sexiest little groan.

"Please, Derek. Please. I need it." Now that she was here, she knew she couldn't get off his lap without it. All the floggings she'd had from Simon had done the job, but there hadn't been a well of emotion flowing between them. There was friendship and competence, not this deep need she could feel coming from Derek. How long had it been since the Dom giving her discipline needed her as much as she needed him?

She felt it. That little baby draft of air and then the loud *smack* that followed, and she couldn't help it. She reached for his ankles, grabbing on more because she needed the connection to him than the balance. She wanted it all of a sudden, wanted more than the friendly exchange of service for service. She wanted to need someone, and though it was a bad idea that man was Derek, she didn't care in that moment.

He smacked her ass again, sending that sweet burn through her skin. "That's right. Hold on to me. Let me know how it feels. Are you with me?"

"Yes, Sir." She kept her voice low because he'd told her to keep it down. The hum of activity on the outside would likely mask the' smacks, but if she called out, there would probably be ten of Dallas's finest trying to break down the door.

*Smack. Smack.* The pain sparked along her skin, causing her to tense at first. It was just pain in the beginning, but she knew what came after. For the patient sub there was pleasure at the end, as though the body could reward her for hanging in there.

Derek wasn't a softie. Tears dripped from her eyes as he laid into her backside. Over and over. She wanted to cry out, but she kept her mouth shut and let herself go.

This was what she missed. She didn't have to think here. She didn't have to worry about falling off the wagon or feel regret for all the things she'd done as a kid. She didn't miss anyone when she was in this place. She simply was. She simply endured and felt and let herself be. Peace, a blessed peace, came with the pain. It didn't for everyone. She knew that. But it worked for her, and she'd learned long ago to accept herself.

She lost count, didn't care after a while. The tears were a release of all the horrible tension of the day, the last few weeks, really. Though she didn't scream out her pain, just the act of crying felt like someone had opened a valve inside her soul and released all the noxious emotions that had built up there—that she wasn't worthy, that everything that had happened was her fault, that she'd always be alone and deserved nothing less.

All the pain she held inside on a daily basis seemed to leech away as he spanked her.

Finally, after the sweetest forever, his hand stilled on her cheeks. His palm covered her, holding the heat to her skin. He was back to caressing her.

"You did well. God, you're fucking gorgeous like this, Karina. Your skin. It's so beautiful."

Spoken like a true Dom. The Doms she knew loved to see their marks on a sub, loved to see a pink ass and know it was there because of their discipline. Something about the way Derek spoke seemed to go straight to her soul. She'd never heard him talk to a sub intimately. He'd always seemed like one of those distant Doms who never let an ounce of emotion flow, but there was such heat in his voice that it melted all of her inhibitions. It was so different than their one hurried and ungainly scene. This time she connected with him. She let her body sag on his, her legs spread just the tiniest bit because her backside wasn't the only thing that was hot and pink. Her pussy had responded to him by softening and getting ripe and ready for his touch.

She heard a shaky breath escape from his mouth and his finger ran down the seam of her ass.

Time seemed to still as he moved closer and closer to her pussy. So close. He would touch her and suddenly she was terrified that she would go off like a rocket the minute he did. The very second those callused fingers of his breached her long unused pussy, she would very likely scream and moan and come all over his hand. She wouldn't say a word if he shoved her on the desk, pushed his slacks down, and took her. She would let him. It had been so long. So fucking long.

He moved his fingers away. She bit back a cry because she'd wanted him to touch her so badly and now it was over and it hadn't been enough. Not even close. He would set her on her feet and she would awkwardly pull her pants up and they would go on like he'd never spanked her, never held her down and made her cry. They would go right back to being wary acquaintances. She would be back in the world and she wasn't ready for it yet.

He flipped her over like she didn't weigh a thing, settling her on his lap. "Relax. I want to play for a minute. You can tell me no, but I don't shift quickly. I like to spend a little time in aftercare before I have to go back to normal. You can stop me at any time with a simple no."

His hand was at the exposed portion of her thigh, skimming up toward her pelvis. Even more disconcerting was the little nest his arm and chest made. He'd situated her so she was oh so close to his body, her head naturally resting against his shoulder, nestling into his neck until she could smell the soap on his body, the clean smell of his skin. She brushed her forehead against his cheek, feeling the roughness of his whiskers against her.

"I like you like this, Karina. Soft. Sweet. I even like the way your jeans hold your legs together. I'd bind you up and then I would have to work to get at your pussy, but don't think I won't. I could tie you up so tight and I would still find a way to get inside you."

He was almost there. She couldn't stop the way she shivered in his arms because it was so much more intimate this way. She was so close to him. His cock pressed against her still-sensitive backside. His lips hovered above hers. All it would take was a slight twist of his head and his mouth would cover hers, his tongue licking along the seam of her lips as his fingers played in her pussy.

"We can work together, Karina. We can make this work," he murmured as he turned his face down.

Like gravity calling to her, she moved with him. Her legs opened as much as they could, her lips turning up to meet his.

They could make this work. They could be good for each other.

A loud knock cracked through the air.

Karina was jarred back to reality and practically jumped off his lap. Her heart was pounding, her whole body aching for something that wasn't going to happen. Oh, god, she'd been just about to spread her legs and let a man who didn't even like her inside. Years and years of chastity and faithfulness to her husband's memory had almost blown out the door.

Tears blurred her eyes. She'd almost kissed another man.

Derek caught her around her waist before she fell over. "Hey, baby, it's all right. The door's locked."

She shook her head. "Don't. You can't call me that."

She'd been Kevin's baby. Sometimes she could still hear him calling her baby and telling her everything would be all right. She forced back tears. She'd been naked with Doms at Sanctum, but none of it had touched her the way the last few minutes with Derek had. Not in all the floggings and spankings and demos had she ever once laid in the Dom's arms and reveled in how he smelled and how his arms had sheltered her.

For just a few seconds, she'd felt safe.

Derek stepped back and his face went to that blank mask she knew so well. "Of course. You should get dressed, Karina. I'll be at your place tonight at six to go over the specifics of the case. If Sean and Liam have to leave, call me and I'll arrange to leave here early. I don't want you alone."

She managed to get her jeans up and with shaking hands, pulled the zipper. What had she just done?

Derek reached over his desk and pulled a box of tissue. He handed it to her with the politeness of a stranger. "You're crying."

She probably looked horrible. She wasn't a pretty crier. Unlike a lot of other women she knew who could look gorgeous when they teared up, she inevitably went a blotchy red and her face puffed up. She grabbed the box, taking a couple of tissues. "Thank you."

"Derek! I know you're in there, lover. Open the door," a feminine voice demanded.

Karina felt her eyes go wide as she looked back at Derek.

It seemed to be his turn to go red. "It's my ex and she is most certainly not my lover, Karina, so wipe the indignation off your pretty face and you might want to flee. She's a raving beast underneath all that Prada."

She huffed a little. She knew exactly what she looked like when she'd been crying. "You don't have to be mean. I know I look terrible."

He frowned and his hand came out to force her to look at him. "You're beautiful when you cry because I know you mean it. You cry like a woman, not a manipulative little girl. It pleases me, Karina, and at least for the next few weeks, I hope that means something to you. Now go home and don't look her in the eyes. She's like Medusa. She will turn you to stone."

And *she* was apparently impatient. There was another volley of knocking. "Derek! I'm not kidding. Quit fucking whoever you're fucking and open the damn door."

"She sounds lovely." Karina forced herself to stop shaking. It wasn't Derek's fault that she felt so damn guilty. He'd done everything he should have done. He'd given her every out. Well, he'd also threatened to take her off the case, but she could almost forgive him for that. He was an old school "protect the women" kind of guy. It was just she was pretty sure up until today, he hadn't considered her a woman.

God, he'd made her feel like one.

She winced as she caught sight of his previously pristine slacks. "Oh, Derek, I am so sorry. Your pants are…"

He looked down and she was deeply surprised to hear him chuckle. There was a stain on his pants from her arousal. She'd made a hell of a wet spot. Derek always seemed so staid. She'd expected him to get angry, but he merely righted his shirt and readjusted himself. "Next time I'll remember just how wet you get, Karina."

The knocking became a staccato nuisance.

"Hold your freaking horses, lady. He's coming out in a minute." Whoever his ex was, she was rude.

Derek frowned her way. Derek didn't do rude.

Karina shrugged as she made her way to the door. "Sorry."

"Remember what I said about the eyes." His voice seemed so much warmer than before. "And I'll expect you to be waiting for me, Karina. I'll call and get your dinner order and pick it up for us. We have work to do."

In for a penny… "I'll cook."

His face twisted slightly as though he was trying not to contemplate something horrible. "You will?"

Bastard. So he didn't think she could possibly cook. Well, she wasn't going to defend herself. Sometimes showing was way better than telling. "Yes, I will. Dinner is at seven."

She opened the door, expecting to see some gorgon of a woman, but the female who was pacing outside Derek's door was petite and perfect, with a fashionably slim figure and icy blonde hair that likely never went frizzy. She wore a gorgeous suit that managed to be both business-like and deeply feminine. There was a fragility to her features that would have every man in a two-mile radius panting after her. It was easy to see this was a woman who spent an enormous amount of time on her body. She likely spent hours on her hair and makeup and the perfect nails on her gorgeous hands. A pampered woman who tried to please the men around her with her looks.

Karina didn't bother to look at her own nails. Unless she was going to Sanctum, she didn't bother with things like makeup and nails. Her hair was in a ponytail because her job often had her running after people or running from them.

She would bet the woman in front of her had never chased a bounty through a junk yard or gone through someone's garbage to figure out if they were hiding a kidnapped kid in their house.

This was the woman Derek had married, his ideal. She was so far from Karina that they weren't even playing in the same league.

He really was looking for a delicate flower he could take care of. Karina wasn't petite and fragile. She'd been on her own for a very long time. She would never be more than a convenient good time for Derek Brighton.

"Is there a problem?" Delicate Flower asked, staring at Karina like she didn't have a brain in her head. She'd placed a hand on her slender hip and frowned Karina's way like she was a bit of refuse someone had forgotten to take out.

Karina shook her head. "Not at all. He's all yours."

The ex-Mrs. Brighton's perfect lips curled in a Cheshire Cat grin. "He always is. You should probably know that before you go and lose your sad little cop heart to the big bad lieutenant. He has a bad habit of fucking below his station, but he always comes back to me."

And just like that Karina's insecurities were swept away in a tidal wave of pure pissed-off. She didn't like mean girls. Mean girls made the world a worse place. "I'm not a cop. I'm a PI."

Cool blue eyes rolled. "Like I care, though that's way worse."

She strolled into the door of Brighton's office and slammed it in Karina's face.

Karina suddenly knew what she would do with her afternoon. But first she had to figure out what the ex-Mrs. Brighton's name was. It wouldn't take much. The good news was, she was a damn fine hacker and she definitely believed that karma at times needed a good shove in the right direction.

If the delicate flower liked to play Medusa, maybe Karina could take on the role of Perseus. It was really for the good of all womankind that she slay the gorgon.

"Hey, Keller? Can I use your computer?" She walked up to the sergeant who hired her from time to time to check out his daughter's dates. Dani Keller unfortunately had a bad-boy complex that got her in trouble every now and then. She was a sweet kid. Karina had been more than happy to help keep her that way.

"Sure. You gonna fuck with someone?" He stood up, offering her his seat.

"I would never do that," Karina assured with a smooth smile.

She was a good liar and this would take her mind off the very dangerous door she'd almost opened with Derek.

It was a door that had to stay closed.

# Chapter Three

"God, Derek, are you slumming or what? Tell me you weren't actually doing something sexual to whatever it was that just walked out of your office."

Just the sound of her voice made his blood go a little cold. He'd had a massive erection, but the sound of her voice was like reverse Viagra. His dick damn near curled up on itself. The Ice Princess, Queen Bitch of the World, strode into his office.

Karina hadn't been cold. She'd almost melted his skin when he touched her. It had been a revelation. He'd expected her to tease him, to use her beauty to its best advantage by attempting to manipulate him, but there had been zero artifice in Karina's argument. It was unexpected and utterly refreshing. There had been a sweetness in the way she'd settled herself over his lap, offering herself up to him.

He'd spanked Karina and felt more in those few moments than he had in the last several years.

"Derek? Are you listening to me?"

He'd kind of hoped if he ignored her she would go away—like a dinosaur that couldn't see you if you didn't move. It was a pipe dream so maybe honesty would work. "No, I'm not listening to you. I'm thinking about how close I came to getting inside Karina. It's five years after our divorce and you're still responsible for my not getting laid."

He sat behind his desk with a long sigh.

Maia's eyes narrowed. "Well, it looks like she left her mark on you. Jeez, Derek. What happened to your pants?"

He couldn't help the smile that crossed his face. Actually it felt more like the goofy grin of a teenaged boy who finally got his hands on a boob. It was stupid. She wasn't his type, wasn't anything close to what he wanted in a permanent submissive much less another wife, and yet the thought of her biting that lip while she decided whether or not to submit to him got his blood hot all over again. "Don't worry about that. Why are you here?"

Maia frowned and turned to look at the closed door as though she could see through it. "You're really fucking that low-grade PI? Derek, what the hell is wrong with you? If you're that hard up, I will find you a date. We have some very submissive interns. I swear, there's a pretty brunette who pees a little when you yell at her. I'm sure you could train that out of her. Her father is a circuit court judge. He can help you out enormously. She's got nice tits and they're totally real."

And Maia would know because she'd very likely slept with her. Maia didn't discriminate when it came to her sexual partners. She was an omnivore. Derek was certain she'd probably sleep with a goat if she found one attractive and it could help her career.

"I'll take a hard pass. Why are you here besides the fact that you outed me to brass?" It didn't look like it was actually going to cost him his job, but then she hadn't known that, had she?

It surprised him a little since Maia was a bitch from hell, but she'd never been truly malicious with him. Yes, she'd cheated on him on a regular basis, but she'd strangely always had his back when it came to work. They'd always been a successful team. He'd just wanted so much more than to be a team member.

Well, and he'd also kind of wanted to not be cheated on with every man he knew.

Maia's face softened as much as the Botox in it allowed as she leaned against his desk. "Brass is all a bunch of perverts, Derek. Trust me, successful people all tend to be perverts. Unsuccessful people, too. And the ones who aren't are fooling themselves. I have enough on the chief to ensure that you move up when you want to move up. All you have to do is say the word and I'll make it happen."

And that was Maia to a T. Always making a deal, always working an angle. She would likely be the Dallas District Attorney before she was forty. "I'll handle my own career, thank you. You had no right to go to them. You should have come to me and asked me if I wanted to be involved."

She shook her head with a long-suffering sigh. "And if I came to you with four dead girls, one of them a cop in this precinct, are you telling me you would have turned down the assignment so no one would know you like to spank subs? Should I have gone straight to Ian? I'm totally not going to do that because he's an asshole."

"No. I would have gone to them myself. I would have offered my services." She was forever cutting his balls off. Even though he hadn't touched her since long before the divorce, she was still making decisions for him, decisions that shouldn't be hers.

"So I saved you a step. Chill out. You're acting like I tried to kill you when all I did was give you the biggest opportunity of your career. Can't you see how good this is going to be? For both of us?"

And just like that it all fell into place. "You're handling the case."

She shrugged a little. "I did put together the team. I do know the lifestyle. I outed myself, too, Derek. The DA thinks this case would best be handled by a female, and I was going to make damn sure I was the female. Besides the only other chick who can handle a case like this is Marian Greeley, and she's sixty-five with a face like a horse. She is so not ready for TV. She would likely say the girls had it coming because she's a dried up old prune who thinks sex is evil. It had to be me. It's best for the victims. So, see, I didn't shove you out alone into shark-infested waters. Consider me your life jacket."

A life jacket that would likely strangle him in her deep need to get ahead. "You still had no right."

"We'll have to agree to disagree on that. Now what's your plan? I want you to coordinate with me. This is the rarest of cases, Derek. This is a serial case the feds haven't taken yet. Bastards. We need to solve this and fast because at some point they will figure out how hot this case is, move in, and we'll lose all our control. The Rangers are willing to work with us because apparently their kinks aren't the same as ours and they're really high on Eve St. James."

"McKay. She remarried."

"Hmmm, well, that's nice. I suppose that means McKay's on the case, too." She grimaced a little. "Did the Rangers bring in Ian? Because he hates me."

"You're in luck. Big Tag's in Europe."

She breathed a sigh of relief. "Oh, thank god. The last time I applied for membership at Sanctum, he put me through a ton of paperwork and when he sent me the letter that would state the date I could start it simply said when hell freezes over. Jerk, though I suppose he's loyal to you."

He would have to send Big Tag a bottle of Scotch. The last thing he needed was to have his club invaded by Maia. "Back to the case, please?"

"Fine. So is Eve working on a profile? Tell her to come to my office when it's done. I don't want that profile leaking to anyone. If the feds get it they'll swoop down and scoop up all my work and take all my glory. I hate them."

Derek felt his eyes narrow. She only ever got truly angry over one thing. "Who turned you down?"

The slightest hint of pink hit her cheeks. "No one turns me down. Well, mostly. I might have been dating one of the SACs. He turned out to be an asshole and now he's out for some kind of revenge."

"What did you do?" Because there was no way she was innocent.

"Nothing. Absolutely nothing." A little huff came from her chest. "I might have given his son a blow job. You can't blame me for that. You should have seen him. He's a college quarterback with the tightest ass I've ever seen on a man. He'd just won a bowl game. If you really think about it, I was taking one for the state of Texas. We owe the kid."

"You're a sexual predator, you know." A barracuda with a vagina that sucked up all the air around it. Actually that was a much better analogy. Her vagina was a black hole from which no man escaped. Or woman.

"I refuse to apologize for my appetites." She stood up and paced, her heels clacking against the floor. "Are you going to be difficult?"

"About the case? No. It's important." For many reasons, the chief one being protecting Karina, but he didn't want to put her on Maia's radar by mentioning that. It was irrational since Karina was every bit as tough as Maia, but he didn't want Maia to hurt Karina. She could be brutal when she thought another woman was threatening her place. Not that she had a place with him. She simply had a delusional belief that they were still some sort of a team. It was just habit. They'd known each other since they were kids in elementary school. Sometimes he sat and talked to Maia just because she was the only one around who remembered what he'd been like before. Before adulthood. Before the war. Even before their divorce.

She sighed and moved to the chair in front of his desk. "Good, because this is the one, Derek. This is the one that moves us both up. If you can crack this case, you could move over to the Rangers if you want to, though I think you're better off where you are. If you really want to be a bastard, tightwad asshole, we might even be able to talk to the feds about a job. They don't all hate me."

He was getting a headache. "I like my job, Maia. I'll work with you on this, but I'm not doing it because I want some magical promotion. Some cops do the job because it's the right thing to do. Some of us enjoy actually doing the work and solving the case because it brings someone justice, not because it might increase our paychecks."

He could hear Tag complaining about how mercenary Karina was. It would be a good thing for him to remember. She might seem soft and sweet when she was in his arms, but she got every dime she could out of her clients. She wasn't that far off from Maia and when she looked for a Dom, she would likely choose one with the most upwardly mobile potential.

"Oh, that is so very Captain America," Maia said with a sad shake of her head. "You should be happy I look out for you."

"I would be way happier if you completely left me alone."

"Sure you would." She crossed her legs seductively and gave him a wink.

She was a gorgeous woman and he had nothing for her. On the outside, she was his type. Oh, she could eat a cheeseburger or two, but she took care of herself. Her hair was perfect, her nails always a sexy red. There was something about the thought of a woman performing all those little beauty rituals that got his motor running. Maia was perfect on the outside but it was Karina he couldn't stop thinking about.

"Are you really fucking the PI?" She leaned forward, her eyes on him.

"It's none of your business, Maia."

"It's just she's not your usual."

"Again, not your business."

"You're never going to forgive me, are you?"

In a lot of ways he really had. He'd made his share of mistakes, too. No marriage was completely one sided. "You are who you are, Maia."

"I love you more than I love almost anything, Derek." She sat back and gave him a little smile. "I just love me way more. But I still watch your back even though I know you call me Medusa behind mine."

"I absolutely do not. I say it to your front." He never prevaricated with her. He didn't have to. It was one of the reasons they'd stayed in this weird friendly enemies state. He didn't have to pretend with Maia.

"Fine, and I'll admit, I kind of like it. Medusa was a woman who knew how to get what she wanted. But even though you rage against me, I still love you and I still want what's best for you and you're never going to be happy until you get married and have some kids. You aren't getting any younger, Derek."

He groaned and wished there would be some sort of tragedy to befall the city so he could get out of this conversation. "Oh, now you sound like my mother."

"Are you the one who told her to make the sign of the cross every time she walks by me at church?"

"Who let you into a church?" Derek chuckled. His mother had a sense of humor. "I'll get her to stop."

Maia waved it off. "Don't worry about it. It gives me a certain reputation I find helpful. So is the thing with the PI serious?"

She wouldn't give up until he told her something. Maia annoyed the hell out of him, but he couldn't forget that she'd been his high school sweetheart. She'd been the one to take care of him when he came back from Afghanistan. She'd been the one who pushed to get him on the force.

When he really thought about it, they had been a good team. They just hadn't been good at being in love.

"It's not. She's part of the operation. Her name is Karina Mills."

Maia's mouth dropped open. "Wait. Are you talking about the girl set to get strangled next?"

He really didn't like it being put that way. "She's been identified as the next target. I intend to make sure she stays safe."

"By putting your dick in her?" She held up a hand, stopping him from ordering her out of his office. "I'm sorry. I'm sorry. I can't help but be a little jealous. I'm your wife after all."

"Ex."

"For you, maybe, but you'll always be my husband. I'm not getting married again. We both know it's not my gig. So you like the PI, who needs a manicure by the way. And she could use some fashion advice. She's not your type, Derek."

A pounding headache was starting to sink in. "Which is why it's a good thing I'm not dating her."

"Or it could be a good thing because the type of woman you're looking for doesn't exist."

"What's that supposed to mean?"

She frowned, her lips a stubborn line. "It means I'm tired of watching you fuck this up. You need to stop looking for this perfect sub of yours and let yourself fall in love with a real woman with real flaws who could potentially really adore the man you are. You deserve that, but you have it in your head that if you control every aspect of the relationship, nothing can go wrong. It's a lie. You know damn well things can go wrong even when you love someone so much it hurts inside because at the end of the day, we're all screwed up. Some of us more than others. I hate saying this, but you have to let me go."

He frowned. She couldn't possibly think that was the problem. "I am not pining over you."

Cool blue eyes rolled. "I know that, babe. You're raging at me. You're still so angry with me you can't see straight. We had something good and then we didn't, and that's my fault and your fault and time's fault." She took a deep breath. "Look, I know why you refused marriage counseling. It was over. It couldn't be fixed, but there were things we should have talked about."

"I don't think we had anything to talk about, Maia."

She ignored him and moved on. "You were gone for so long and then you came back a different person and while you were gone, I became a different person. I know Afghanistan changed you, but there were things that changed me, too, and I don't regret any of it with the singular exception of how it hurt you. I have what I want. I know it's weird to think that a job can really make a person happy, but it does for me. Crushing the people under me makes me so happy. Some of us are just born villains and some villains find themselves by accident. But you, you are one of the good guys, and I would hate to see you alone for the rest of your life because you can't look past the one thing that didn't work."

But it had been so much more than one thing. More than his marriage. It wasn't his marriage he saw in his nightmares. And he'd never reached out to her, not after he'd come home from the war. He'd fucked her, told himself he loved her, but she was right. He had been a different man than the one she'd stood beside at the altar at the stupid age of eighteen.

What she didn't understand was that he wasn't looking for love anymore. He was looking for companionship and sex and a little peace. Love was a myth he'd left behind a long time ago.

"I'll take it under advisement." He would say anything to get rid of her.

"Sure you will. Well, you can't say I didn't try." She stood up. "I'll get back to punching puppies. Who am I kidding? Puppies are cute. That's what interns are for. And seriously, I can get you a date with Subby Cathy."

Her cell trilled and Derek sent a silent thank you to whoever was calling her. The minute she got back to work mode, she would forget about trying to fix his life.

Her face went bright red. "What do you mean they towed my Benz? Damn it. I am not behind on my payments. I own that fucking car. I am going to ruin someone. You tell them to stop. I don't care what you have to do. Throw your body in front of the truck. Offer the man a blow job. What do you mean he's already gone?"

She was screaming into her cell as she stormed from the room.

Just as the door closed, he noticed Karina sitting at Keller's desk. She looked up from the computer she absolutely shouldn't be using and the sexiest, most evil grin split her face as Maia stomped by. Yeah, he shouldn't have been worried. Karina didn't need him to protect her from Maia. She could do that all on her own.

He was surrounded by crazy bitches. He didn't even want to know what Karina had done to get Maia's car towed.

The door closed and Derek was left in blissful silence. He knew he had to change his pants before he made his meeting with the captain, but he sat for a moment, letting the scent of Karina's arousal relax him.

There was something oddly peaceful about it.

# Chapter Four

Karina turned into her Deep Ellum apartment complex and cursed the day her building decided to go all egalitarian on the parking spaces. Karina had only heard the rumor that there had been assigned parking at one time, but it was a dream. She groaned as she drove past the aisle closest to her and then decided to give it up. She always ended up in the damn back.

She parked her Jeep and grabbed the groceries she'd bought. She hoped the lieutenant liked chicken and dumplings because she was in need of some comfort food.

He was coming over. To her apartment. Had she cleaned? She kept the place fairly neat, but sometimes when she was working a case things got a little disorganized. A lot disorganized. She glanced at her watch. Five thirty. Derek had texted her he was leaving work early. She had a whole thirty minutes before he got here. She needed to clean up, wipe down the countertops, maybe get rid of the boxes of old Chinese food that had been decorating the shelves of her fridge for way longer than they should have.

Maybe she should put on some lip gloss. She should definitely change. Or should she? She was just going to cook. She wouldn't want to get sauce all over her clothes. Did she even own an apron? Definitely lip gloss and maybe some mascara.

*Stop. Halt. Cease that line of thought.*

She just managed to not trip on the curb as she walked toward the door to her building. She couldn't think that way. This wasn't some date. Brighton wasn't coming over for dinner and a movie and a heavy make-out session. He was coming over because they were working together and the minute the case was over, he would be out of her life, so she needed to be a smart girl and stay the fuck off his lap. Even though it had been a ridiculously nice lap. He had the sort of lap made for a sub to spend hours over with her bare ass in the air.

Some Dom's laps were all knees and bony thighs, but Brighton had strong legs. He was big enough that she'd been comfortable lying there.

And the way he'd manhandled her afterward. He'd just picked her up and flipped her over without a single strain in those muscular arms of his. For that one moment, she'd felt delicate and lovely and petite against him. She wasn't a small girl. Never had been. She'd always carried a little extra weight, but Derek hadn't seemed to notice.

She stopped in front of the door and took a long breath. Liam and Sean were still in her apartment. She couldn't walk inside all hot and bothered. They weren't dumb men. They would know what had happened, and she really wanted to keep that private.

A little glint came off the door handle as she went to open it and Karina stopped, all thoughts of Brighton fleeing in an instant.

She was being watched. Yes, that little glint of light could have come from the sun hitting the metal in the early evening, but she doubted it. It had been the faintest hint and was gone in an instant. If there had been anyone else in the parking lot, she would have thought it was someone opening and shutting their car doors, the mirror catching the light and reflecting it to the handle she held.

Or someone was using binoculars and they had briefly caught the sun.

Karina always followed her instincts. She'd learned far too often that things went poorly when she didn't. Oh, sometimes they turned out to be wrong, but it was way better to be safe than sorry.

Someone was watching her and she needed to get to a place where he couldn't. As calmly as she could, she opened the door and strode inside, walking for the elevator that would take her to her floor. Her heart was racing, adrenaline starting to pump in anticipation, but she took a deep breath to try to quash it. She couldn't go after him at this point. If she turned and looked around, trying to figure out where the watcher was, she would definitely tip the fucker off that she was on to him. If he had half a brain, he knew she was a PI. While he might find the chase exciting, he also might back off and go after weaker prey if she showed strength too soon in their game.

The elevator dinged and she got in, pressing the button for the tenth floor.

How much did the unsub know about her? How much had he known about any of his victims? Had he known Amanda was a cop? It was still so difficult to think about her being gone. She hadn't been kind, but Karina wouldn't wish her fate on anyone.

Had the four victims had anything in common beyond their interest in BDSM and attendance at clubs? There had to be something more. The guy had come out of nowhere and suddenly had four kills to his credit. If he was truly a serial killer, he would have killed before, perfecting his method over time.

She needed to read Eve's profile.

The door opened and she walked to her apartment, already thinking up a million and one arguments in case Derek tried to keep the profile confidential. She wasn't going to be left out. If she was a member of the team, then she was going to force him to treat her like one.

She opened the door and walked inside. Of course, Derek could see arguing as disobeying his rules, and she would find herself over that supercomfy lap of his, taking his discipline. His cock would pulse against her belly almost as if it were connected to his hand, both finding a rhythm of arousal that would get her hot and wet in an instant.

"Karina? Did you run up the stairs?" Liam O'Donnell stood in her living room, shaking his head like a disappointed father who caught his daughter coming in after curfew. "Because you're flushed. Otherwise I might wonder why you're blushing."

"Yep. Gotta get in my exercise." She lied without a single qualm. Settling the groceries on the counter of her small kitchen, she frowned at the layer of dust she found there. How long had it been since she'd actually been in the kitchen?

"Liar," the Irishman shot back. "I put a camera on the stairs. You came up the lift. So what's that blush about, girl? Brighton already making you crazy?"

There was a low laugh as Sean Taggart stepped out of her bedroom. "Ten bucks says Brighton's already gotten her naked. At least partially. The last time I saw him, he was ushering her into his office and shutting all the blinds."

Li shook his head. "Karina isn't giving in so easy."

"Karina isn't giving in at all," she said, completely unwilling to go into her love life with two men who treated her like a kid sister. "Karina is working a case and unlike the two of you, I know how to keep business and pleasure separate."

Let them stew on that for a while. They had both met their spouses during ops.

Li's eyes widened. "Shit. You already let him play."

Sean laughed as Karina shook her head. "Don't even try it. You always get prissy when you're trying to deflect. And I can smell the bastard's aftershave on you from here."

*Shit and balls.* "He was just trying to prove a point and it wasn't really play. It's undercover work." Luckily she had the perfect thing to get them off the subject. "I think our guy is watching me. You two need to be careful."

A single eyebrow rose on Sean's face, a move he seemed to have gotten from his brother. Or maybe the ability to make a person feel like a dumbass with a single look was just in the Taggart DNA. "And you're mentioning this now? That might have been a good reason to use your phone."

When Little Tag wanted to Dom out, he could go all the way. Luckily he wasn't her Dom. "I was already on my way up and I didn't want to tip the bastard off. The last thing I want to do is spook the guy. We need him to come after me."

Sean stared her way. "Fine. What direction did it seem to come from?"

"If I had to bet, he was in the building across the street," she said. "It's got easy access and if he needed to he could be here in a couple of minutes or get on the train and be gone in the same time."

Li groaned a little. "I don't like it. I don't like any of it. I don't like working with government employees. They put covering their asses over solving the case. I definitely don't think we should be using Karina as bait. If a damn thing goes wrong they'll cut her loose and she'll be just another dead body."

Li had serious issues with authority—particularly government bodies—but then they had burned him in the past. She had to admit it was nice that somebody didn't want her to end up stuffed in a body bag.

"No, she won't because we're going to look after her," Sean said. "We're her backup. Besides, Derek won't let anything happen to her and he won't give a shit about red tape. It's the only reason I'm not calling in favors to get her shoved into protective custody."

Karina rolled her eyes. "What's up with you guys and protective custody? I'm not exactly fragile. I can hold my own. You guys have sent me into plenty of tight spots."

"Not without backup," Li replied. "We run ops differently than the government. Our people come first and we don't have to answer to anyone about it. Derek has to answer to his captain and the chief. The department has to answer to the Rangers. Everyone has to liaise with the fucking DA. It's a maze of shit, I tell you."

It probably was, but she wasn't going to worry about it. She had Sean and Liam as her backup. They wouldn't give a crap what the press would say, and no one would fire them if they chose her well-being over the op. "Well, I'm willing to listen to the two of you. You might have to fight with Brighton, though. Apparently his ex-wife is the ADA on the case."

She'd spent an hour researching the ex-Mrs. Brighton.

"Shit," Sean said. "Maia is a raging bitch half the time and a succubus forty-nine percent of the time."

She'd kind of figured that out. Keller had been more than willing to talk about the ex-Mrs. Brighton. "And the remaining one percent?"

Sean shrugged. "She has moments of kindness. Brief moments. They're usually followed by someone getting fired. Anyway, just let Derek handle her. Now, we've got some security set up. Like Li said, we put a couple of small cameras in the stairs. The elevators already have cameras and there are setups at each of the entrances that we hacked into so we'll have someone watching. Is there a reason there's no keyed entry to the building?"

"You need a key fob to get into the gate to the lot, but too many people complained about having to buzz in their friends." It wasn't exactly a hot spot for crime, but Dallas wasn't some fuzzy suburb either. "Of course, all a person really has to do is wait until someone comes in or out and they can drive right through."

"Or walk up." Li leaned against her counter. "Why the hell are you here, Karina? There are far nicer places with better security."

"I can't afford them. I don't work for some big corporation with endless pockets." She grinned a little. "Tag is my biggest client and I overcharge the hell out of him so I can work for the little guys. Most of my clients can't pay me crap, but it doesn't mean they don't need me. It does mean that I can't afford a big nice place. This is stretching my budget as it is."

Sean snorted a little. "I knew there was a reason I loved you, K. You keep sticking it to big brother. I'll never tell."

Liam chuckled. "You always were one to fight the good fight, love. Now let's talk about how to ease ourselves into your daily life."

They were worried that the unsub would figure out something was wrong if she suddenly had a bunch of men in her life. It made sense. If he'd been watching her for any amount of time, he'd likely seen a woman who worked and went to clubs and not a whole lot else. "I thought you were going to work at one of the clubs. Can't I meet you there?"

"Alex had an in. He got me a job as a bartender at the club we're most interested in. Li's going in as a bouncer. I don't want to overtax our resources so we're going to put our emphasis on that club. Three of the four victims had been known to play there. But I think we need a story about why Li and I come in and out of your place so often, and you need to stick with it with anyone who doesn't know the truth. I mean anyone, Karina."

"That wouldn't be a whole lot of people, guys," Karina admitted. "I work most of the time. The people at Sanctum are pretty much the whole of my social group."

"Good," Liam said. "The less people we have to deal with, the better."

There was a knock on her door.

Sean frowned. "I thought you said you didn't have friends."

She shrugged. "Maybe it's Brighton. He said he was coming over. He's early though."

Karina crossed the small space to the door and opened it, expecting to see the big gorgeous cop who she was absolutely, one hundred percent not going to sleep with. Her mouth dropped open. "Terry?"

Her brother-in-law stood in the doorway, grinning from ear to ear. He was a younger version of Kevin in the face, though he was much more slender in build than her husband had been. "Hey, Karina. Bet you're surprised to see me."

Well, that threw a big old wrench into her plans. "You could say that."

He held up his arm, and Karina could see the beginnings of a cast wrapped around his hand. The rest was in a long-sleeved shirt, but she could see the outline of the cast went almost to his elbow. "Come on. Let me in. I'm injured. I only have a couple of minutes until I have to go see my therapist. He's just up the road a bit, so I thought I'd stop by to let you know I'm in town."

She shook her head, completely in shock. She hadn't seen Terry in years, hadn't even spoken to him in almost six months. Terry was the only one left from Kevin's family besides some distant cousins and uncles and aunts, who hadn't been close. He was older than she remembered, thinner. "Of course. What happened to your arm?"

He sighed as he stepped inside. Her small apartment was getting crowded. "The usual. I was in the Caribbean making a little cash by taking the tourists deep sea fishing. They got drunk and harassed the girl I had serving drinks. Asshole broke my arm. Needless to say I'm no longer welcome at the Bermuda Fisherman's Club. I have a friend who's a therapist here. I'm staying with him while I rehab." He turned and caught sight of Liam and Sean. "And you have friends over. Wow. I didn't expect that."

She felt herself flush. There was no way to miss the disapproval in his voice. It was stupid, but the idea of Kevin's brother thinking she was screwing around really made her nervous. It was almost like Kevin finding out. Utterly irrational, but she found herself floundering. "Guys, this is Terry Mills. He's Kevin's brother. Terry, uhm, this is…"

Sean's face went from hard to smooth in a heartbeat and he stepped up. "Her very good friend. I'm Sean. This is my boy, Li. I would call him my husband, but we're not allowed to do that in the state of Texas. It's a shame you know because our wedding would be fabulous."

Liam stared at Sean. "Are ya kidding?"

Sean rolled his eyes negligently. "Don't mind him. He doesn't want to spend the money on a wedding. He's a tightwad. So you're Karina's brother-in-law? I have to admit we've been curious about our girl's family."

Holy freaking shit. Sean had picked his cover and it looked like Liam hadn't been in on the plan. If she hadn't been in a sticky situation, she would have poured herself a tea and sat back and watched the fireworks. As it was, all she could manage was to nod her head. "Yes, this is Terry Mills. He's Kevin's younger brother."

Terry sighed and laughed a little. "Sorry. For a minute there I thought Karina was dating again. That was a shocker."

Sean grinned and gave her a little wink. He was actually really good at that. He should have gone into theater. "Oh, she is. You should see him. That is one hunk of a man. Isn't he, Li?"

And Liam was a terrible actor. He just frowned. "He ain't exactly my type."

Sean waved him off. "Mr. Grumpy there likes blonds. Lucky for me."

Terry frowned Karina's way. "You have a boyfriend?"

Karina shook her head. Sean had been very specific. He really didn't want to break their cover for anyone, and that meant she had to keep hers, too. Even to what was left of her family. Still, she found she couldn't let him down entirely. "Not really. He's just a guy I met at a club."

Terry went a faint pink and he leaned in, his good hand on hers. "Tell me you aren't still into that scene, Karina. It was dangerous when Kevin was with you. It's insane now. Tell me you aren't playing around with that BDSM crap."

It was her turn to flush. Terry had always had a serious problem with their lifestyle. He could sleep with a girl a night, but he got deeply prudish the minute the handcuffs came out. "It's really none of your business."

"I'm your brother-in-law. I promised Kevin I would look after you if anything happened. It damn straight is my business."

"Then where the bloody hell have you been for the last couple of years? Because I ain't seen anyone looking after her," Liam said, his eyes narrowing.

"I've been working, but I trusted that Karina would be smart enough to stay away from the perverted stuff. I was obviously wrong. Do you know what Kevin would think if he knew you were running around with...what the hell do they call themselves? Doms?" He shook his head and visibly took a breath. "I'm sorry. It's your life, sweetie."

Sean had moved to stand beside her. "It is her life, and I don't know that I like the way you're talking to her."

Terry's eyes narrowed, and Karina remembered how short the fuse on his temper could be. "I don't think you have any say in how I talk to my sister-in-law. You should stay out of family matters."

"Her boyfriend isn't here to defend her so I think I'll stay," Sean said, not giving an inch.

"I can defend myself," Karina said.

"Not in this, you can't." Li shook his head. "You're far too close to this. You've been a widow for years. There's nothing wrong with you dating again."

"But she's not dating, is she? She's getting on her knees for some asshole who wants to make her a slave or some shit," Terry said with a frustrated sigh.

She needed to fix this really fast or Sean and Li would take care of it, and she was pretty sure she wouldn't like how they handled the situation. "Terry, didn't you say you needed to be at the therapist? Maybe I can give you a ride."

He seemed to get hold of his temper. He held his good hand up. "No. I need the exercise. I...I'm sorry, Karina. I didn't mean to walk in and start telling you what to do. I'm just a little surprised to find out you're dating. I guess I still see you with Kevin. You were always Kevin's girl. He did so much for you that I thought you would...I don't know what I thought. I'll get out of your hair."

Tears threatened. She didn't want him to walk out angry with her. Kevin's family had been so good to her. They'd taken her in when she was still shaking from withdrawal. His mom had watched over her while Kevin was working, holding her hand and promising her everything would be all right. She'd taken Karina to church and given her a whole new set of supporters. She'd died before Kevin had. Her last words to Karina were of gratitude for her being the daughter she'd always wanted. Terry was her last link on earth to them. "I'm sorry."

"Me, too," he said as he opened the door. "I'll be around for a few months. Maybe we can have lunch."

She nodded. "I would like that."

He was just about to step through when he turned back. "Hey, I ran into Grant the other day. He said something about finding a box of Kevin's?"

Grant Fisher had been Kevin's partner. She and Kevin had been in the process of moving when he was killed in the line of duty. Grant had graciously offered his attic for some of their stuff while the house on Long Island was being made ready. He'd died before they signed the papers and she'd never walked into that house again. Now Grant was moving and he'd found a couple of boxes she'd missed. "Yes, they're on their way. Do you want to look through them with me?"

Terry nodded, his eyes downcast. "Yeah, that would be nice."

"I'll call you."

And he was gone.

"Hey, sweetheart," Li's arms were going around her. "Don't you listen to a word that bastard said. Ain't nothing wrong with you."

It was easy to sink into Liam's warmth. They'd gone through a lot together. Li seemed to be the one she worked with the most, and he'd taken to treating her like a sister. If Avery had been there, she would have hugged Karina's other side and told Karina to hold her baby because babies made everyone feel better.

She might have lost one family, but somehow she'd found another.

"You know that husband of yours wouldn't want you to live alone the rest of your life," Liam whispered. "That's not the man you described to me. If he loved you, he would want you to be happy. I know I would want Avery to be happy. He wouldn't want you to be so lonely."

"I don't like that little fucker. I'm going to run some checks on him," Sean said.

"Don't, Sean. He's my brother-in-law. He just misses Kevin. Let it go." She gave Liam one last squeeze.

"Am I interrupting something?" a voice that could freeze the sun said from the doorway.

Karina looked up and knew her crappy day wasn't over. Derek was here and he was staring at her like she was a piece of trash.

At least some things never changed.

\* \* \* \*

Derek was surprised at the overwhelming need to take the Irishman and smash his head against Karina's bar. He probably shouldn't though since the whole apartment looked like it was held together with tape and dust. What was she doing here? And what the flying fuck was she doing in Liam O'Donnell's arms?

"Hey, this is no time to unleash your inner Neanderthal. She's had a rough day," Sean said under his breath. He put a hand on Derek's shoulder. "Let her be, okay?"

"So when she's had a rough day, I should let O'Donnell manhandle my sub?" It was actually driving him a little crazy. O'Donnell had played with Karina on more than one occasion. He'd watched them. O'Donnell would be all circumspect on the dungeon floor, giving her a flogging or administering a spanking. He never touched her intimately, but then they would disappear into the bar or hide away in a privacy room and Derek couldn't help but see the handsome Irishman with his hands all over her gorgeous body.

Liam's palms went up like a thief caught red-handed. "She's just me friend, Lieutenant. Don't think there's anything more. Though you should know, I take friendship damn seriously."

He apparently took it more seriously than he did marriage, but then very few people took that seriously these days. Derek forced himself to calm down. It was good that she was already showing her true colors. She was a career-oriented woman who preferred to keep her relationships very casual. Very modern.

Derek nodded Liam's way. "Hey, whatever floats your boat, man. I'm just here for the case. Have we gotten the profile from Eve?"

He moved into Karina's shitastic apartment, avoiding her entirely. She stood there looking at him with a wounded-doe look in those eyes of hers, but he knew it was all for show. Women like Karina didn't get hurt. Not really. She was playing some sort of angle.

He couldn't let himself get in too deep. His every instinct told him to take O'Donnell's place. He should move right in and take her in his arms and explain to her that if she needed comfort, she should come to him. He was her Dom. He was the one who was supposed to be holding her.

Except he wasn't and he never fucking would be, so he checked himself.

"We won't have it until tomorrow," O'Donnell replied. He hadn't moved far from Karina. He was still watching over her like he was waiting for Derek to hurt her.

Karina took a deep breath and seemed to make the decision to change course. She gave him a bright smile. "So you don't have to stay. We can just regroup tomorrow."

Yeah, that wasn't happening. He held up his overnight bag. "I'll stick to my plan, thanks. Do you have a spare bedroom?"

Sean snorted. "She's lucky to have a room big enough for a bed, Derek. There's a reason she never invites anyone over here. I think you're sleeping on the couch, Romeo."

He sent Sean his middle finger and set down his bag since it looked like he would be sleeping in the postage stamp of a living room. "Screw you, Little Tag."

A sexy grin lit Karina's face, and he was so happy it wiped the sorrow from her eyes. "Apparently Sean is going to screw Li, here. They're taking a page from Adam and Jake's playbook. They're going in as a couple. You know you guys are going to have to make people believe it."

The Irishman went a flaming red as he turned to Sean. "You had to go that way, didya?"

Little Tag just shrugged. "Dude, think about it for two seconds. We have to go into a dungeon. We can't walk in with wedding rings on. I don't know about you, but I would prefer to not get hit on. The last thing my wife needs is to worry about younger women. Do you want to go home and tell your wife who just had a baby that you're going to be flirting with a bunch of subs who didn't just have a baby?"

"Shit. I hadn't thought about that. She doesn't have anything to worry about. No one's prettier than my Avery," Liam said.

*Then why the fuck was Liam playing with his sub?*

"Dude, you can tell her that all day. She hasn't lost her baby weight," Karina shot back, completely at ease with the men.

"I don't care if she loses it. She looks amazing," Liam swore. "But I see your point. All right, but I'm the top. I ain't going in as Sean's bloody sub and that's that. If any single one of you thinks that I'm going to let that bastard whip me ass, you don't know me very well."

Karina shrugged a little. "You did say you would do anything it took to make sure I was safe."

"I'm really good at it, Li." Little Tag seemed to have a death wish. "Ask Grace. She says I am an artist with a paddle."

Karina poked at Sean, her utter ease with the men irritating Derek. "Although, I have to admit, Sean came off much more subby. Li was the broody top."

Li held up his fist in jubilation. "That's right. The sub's the expert."

Sean just rolled his eyes. "The good news is we're going to be working and not sceneing." He nodded Derek's way. "But you two better get your stories straight because we go in Saturday night. Spend the time getting comfortable enough that people will believe you two like each other."

"K, come here and show me something." Liam was at her window, pulling up the blinds.

Sean took the opportunity to move into Karina's tiny kitchen, gesturing for Derek to follow. He got the feeling he was going to get a talking to. It looked like Little Tag was serious about standing in for his brother.

"I told you I'm not going to let her die," Derek said quickly, wanting to avoid a lecture from another one of Karina's lovers.

Sean's jaw firmed, his eyes going hard. "Derek, we're friends."

"I like to consider us friends."

"I want to still be friends with you at the end of this. Are you going to fuck her?"

"If it comes up, I probably will." And it would come up. God knew his cock sure as hell came up the minute he thought of her. "What's this about? It's kind of the height of hypocrisy if you're going to warn me about screwing around on the job. Karina is my co-worker. She isn't my target. She knows the score. All she has to do is say no and I'll keep my hands to myself."

Sean shook his head and generally gave Derek the impression that he was deeply irritated. "If I thought you really had the capability of caring about her, I would tell you to go for it in a heartbeat. She's an amazing woman. But you're never going to treat her the way she needs to be treated. You're too fucked up yourself to take care of her."

He felt his pulse rise and wondered if he was about to get into a real fight. "Are you trying to accuse me of something, Sean? I've never abused a sub and I never will."

"You won't hurt her physically, but she's more fragile than she looks. You can rip her apart and you won't even know you've done it because she won't show you anything. Her ex brother-in-law was here right before you came in."

He hadn't known she was married. Well, that was something they had in common. They were both divorced. He wondered what had broken up Karina's marriage and decided he probably didn't want to know. "What does that have to do with anything?"

"His visit upset her. She hadn't seen him in a while and I made the call to start our cover, including telling him that she had a boyfriend," Sean explained.

Derek totally agreed with the call. "The faster we get the cover up, the better. He was upset she's seeing someone?"

"He was a complete dick. He wasn't just nasty about the fact that she's dating. He gave her hell about the lifestyle. Called her perverted and stupid."

Yeah, he definitely needed to check himself. Liam had been doing what any other Dom who cared about her would have done. He was comforting her, reassuring her that there was nothing wrong with her. No matter how he felt about her, he would have done the same. At least he hoped he would have. He'd always treated Karina differently because she was such a threat to his peace of mind. "Did you punch him?"

Sean huffed a little. "Someone already had. The fucker had a broken arm. Look, I'm just worried about her. Like I said, she's more fragile than you think. I can't tell you about her background. I'm not even supposed to know the whole of it, but she's been through a lot."

"Why is she living here? From everything I've heard, she charges out the ass. I kind of thought she was a high-priced PI who worked for whoever paid her the most."

Sean pointed at him. "And that's why I'm afraid. You go to the absolute worst possible answer for a woman like Karina. She charges the hell out of my brother, who likes to complain but who probably knows exactly what she's doing. She then turns around and lets every sad sack with a sob story take advantage of her. She's fighting the good fight, man. She does this for reasons you can't know, but if you really saw her, you would respect the hell out of her. This is a woman you could know. Do you understand me?"

"I know Karina." Though he was starting to wonder. He hadn't expected her to live like this. He'd expected to find her in someplace nicer or at the very least bigger and with way better security.

"No, you don't. So take a few days and get to know her because she's more like you than you can imagine. Just give it a couple of days. Li and I are going to go do a sweep of the area. She thinks she felt someone watching her and K's got great instincts. You keep her safe tonight. One of us will be by in the morning and someone's going to be watching the security at all times." Sean held out a hand. "She's family, Derek."

"I'll take care of her." He shook Sean's hand and wondered how she managed it. What kind of spell did Karina weave that she stayed friends with the men she slept with and even got in good with their wives? What kind of woman did that?

He looked over at her even as he answered his own question. What kind of woman was Karina?

The dangerous kind.

# Chapter Five

Karina sat up in bed, completely unable to sleep because she couldn't stop thinking about the fact that Derek was asleep on her couch.

The whole evening had been oddly comfortable. After Li and Sean had left, Derek had sat on her couch watching a baseball game while she cooked dinner. When he'd popped open a beer, he'd offered her one and he'd stared at her oddly when she refused, but then he'd gone back to casual talk.

They'd talked about the cops they both knew. They'd exchanged a couple of war stories. He'd sat at her bar and eaten three bowls of her homemade chicken and dumplings. She was glad she'd made extra, though originally she'd done it so she could eat the leftovers for a few days. Derek Brighton didn't leave leftovers. The big guy really liked to eat.

But he hadn't touched her. He hadn't even come close. The nearest they'd come to physical contact was their fingers brushing against each other when she'd passed him a pillow.

Her hand still tingled where he'd brushed against her.

She threw back the covers and walked to the window, peeking through the blinds. She couldn't do what she wanted to do. She wanted to open them, open the window, and let the night air in, but some asswipe was out there and everyone would be pissed at her if she did something stupid like make herself a massive target. She couldn't stand the thought of someone watching her.

But damn it, the fucker was screwing up her contemplative process. When she opened the windows and looked out over the city, she could sometimes pretend she was back in New York and she was young with her whole life ahead of her. She could pretend Kevin was just working. She could make believe she'd never opened the door one night and seen Grant's haggard face and known her husband was gone.

But she couldn't throw her blinds up so now all she could think about was Derek and all she could wonder about was how long she was going to hold herself apart.

She wanted him. It would be stupid and pointless to lie to herself. She hadn't wanted another man in years, had comforted the needs of her body with a vibrator she'd actually named and when it had died, she'd cried at that, too. She'd mourned her goddamn vibrator.

She was so screwed up.

There was beer in the fridge. The idea twisted around in her head like a snake ready to bite her. Derek had brought a six pack with him but he'd only had two. There were four cold beers just sitting there, and Derek didn't know enough to get pissed if she drank one. Alcohol had never been her drug of choice. Oh, no. When she went all in, she didn't fuck around. She liked the hard stuff. She liked to stick a needle in her arm.

But the beer might take the edge off.

She let the blind she'd been peeking through slide back down. No. She shoved that thought right back. Soft stuff led to hard stuff and nothing ever really took the edge off.

Life, she'd discovered, was nothing but edges. It was how a person navigated them that meant something.

Karina sat back on her bed, the one that had never seen another person but her. Her lonely bed. Her widow's bed.

She'd enjoyed putting a plate in front of Derek Brighton, enjoyed watching his eyes close in pleasure as he'd eaten, enjoyed the way he sighed and asked for more.

The years had passed and she'd forgotten how good it felt to please someone with her cooking. She ate crap now. She grabbed takeout because it was quick and she didn't have anyone to eat with. She'd forgotten how much better food tasted when she spent time on it and had someone to share it with.

She'd thought she could fill the holes in her heart by helping people, by becoming the PI version of Mother freaking Teresa. The problem was Brighton reminded her of why she could never be a nun.

She was going to a club with him tomorrow. She was going to prance around in her corset and heels and pretend that big gorgeous man was her Dom. She'd promised to obey him, to let him top her. She would be under his command and that thought didn't piss her off the way it should.

Ever since Kevin died, she'd played at D/s. She'd performed scenes, but the minute the scene was done, she'd gone right back to being friends. Sure, Li had taken her to a privacy room a couple of times, but he'd only done that because she'd needed to talk. She hadn't wanted the whole club to see her sobbing and Li was a good listener.

She wasn't sure Derek wanted to listen. Even if he would, she wasn't sure what she would say.

Would she tell him she admired him? Oh, sure there had been that one time when he'd had her arrested for impeding an investigation but she'd totally gotten him back by siccing IA on him.

She shouldn't have done that. *Damn it.* Sometimes her need for justice led her astray. When she really looked back, she was probably in the wrong on that one. She'd been mad at him, but now that she thought about it, she probably had been impeding the investigation. He'd caught the guy even while he'd been dealing with an IA investigation.

He was kind of a hero.

She sighed. He was totally a hero. He'd been a Green Beret and then when he'd come home he'd gone into law enforcement because that was who he was. He was the type of guy who wouldn't be happy unless he knew he was taking care of someone. He needed to protect and serve.

Serve. He could totally serve her. He could service her. He could make her feel so fucking good.

A loud bang made her eyes widen. Adrenaline poured through her system because someone was moving in her living room.

She immediately got to her feet and had a gun in her hand before she could take her next breath. She kept them in a couple of places around the apartment.

Derek. It was Derek. It had to be because she knew damn straight he wouldn't sleep through that. He couldn't. Even as she slunk out of her bedroom door, she knew what she would find.

Derek was still on the couch. His hands were up as though he was fighting. He punched out.

Karina stepped around the lamp that was now on the floor. At least it hadn't broken.

"No. Fucking no." Derek's voice was low, as though he wasn't sure he wanted anyone to hear him.

Her heart skipped a beat. He was caught in something horrible and she stopped. She wasn't some innocent thing. She'd had nightmares of her own and she knew Derek was caught in one. He was lost in some hellhole where the world was set ablaze and he couldn't save anyone or anything.

Her heart damn near broke for him because she understood that piece of Derek Brighton that had eluded her before. He hurt. He ached. When he closed his eyes, he went to Hell.

She knew that feeling. Sometimes, not often anymore, but sometimes when she closed her eyes, she saw herself lying on a toilet, her cheek against the seat. Kevin had found her there. He'd picked her up and carried her out and she'd woken up with a woman she didn't know holding her hand. Her mother-in-law. Kevin had shown up a couple of days later. He'd paid for her rehab. He'd offered her a new life. She'd married him six months later.

Who had been there for Derek?

She took a deep breath and made her decision. She couldn't leave him there. He was stuck in someplace horrible. Yes, he would very likely attack her ass. It was what happened when some dumb girl decided to get involved with PTSD boy, but she couldn't leave him there.

"Derek." She said his name in a firm tone of voice. Karina walked to the bar and set the gun down. She wouldn't need it. The door was locked. The sounds she had heard had all come from Derek. The only true horrors were in his brain. She could handle that.

"No. Fucking no." He grunted the words quietly.

Poor baby boy. Her heart ached for him because she understood. She might not know the hows and whys, but she hurt for him.

"Derek, sweetie, wake up." She reached down to press her finger to Derek's chest in hopes of waking him.

His hand shot out, caging her wrist, dragging her down. "No. Fucking no. No. No. No."

And she was dragged into his Hell. Which would be horrible if she wasn't so competent. She immediately twisted her wrist and dragged her hand away from the big bad Dom.

He seemed to struggle with that. He sat straight up and turned her way, his body aggressive in his pursuit of her. His hand came out, capturing her wrist again and dragging her toward him.

"You don't get to kill me. Do you know what I've fucking been through? Do you think I'll let you have me?" His voice was like gravel, like he hadn't had a drink in weeks.

What had he been through? She knew he'd been stationed in Afghanistan at the beginning of the war.

He needed her. That much was clear. He needed her strength. He needed someone who understood how shitty it had been, not someone who cried and hoped he woke up.

"Derek." She used her best alpha voice.

Derek reached up and grabbed her throat. He was damn fucking serious. She felt every inch of his will.

"No." His hands closed around her.

And she decided to put him on his ass.

Karina dragged him up. She wasn't stupid. She had a few minutes of adrenaline rush plus good training to know how to save herself. She knew just how to work him. She pulled and pushed until he was on the floor in front of her. She took a deep breath as she looked down at him.

"No." Despite the fact that he'd fallen, he was still insistent. He reached up for her. He clawed to get to her. He was determined that she not get away. She let him grasp her wrist, knowing she could free herself at any moment. She had the upper hand. She was fully conscious. She truly understood where she was and he was fighting demons he saw in his nightmares.

"Come on, Brighton. It's time to wake up." She started to squeeze his hand, gently trying to bring him out of the nightmare.

And she found herself on the floor. The big guy was strong even in his sleep.

"No." He held her down with his body, his weight making a cage she couldn't easily break. His chest was against hers.

"Brighton, I don't want to hurt you." But she was beginning to think she would have to.

His hand moved to her throat and his eyes were open now. There was a vacancy in them that disturbed her. He was staring down at her, but obviously not seeing what was right in front of him.

"Hush. You have to be quiet. You have to fucking shut up. You know they're right outside."

"I'll be quiet." She needed to calm him down. She wasn't really afraid of him. Her knee was in the proper position to wake him up very quickly if she had to, but she preferred to help him. He might hold it against her if she shoved his balls into his body cavity.

His head came low. He spoke right into her ear as though he was terrified someone would hear him. "They're right outside that door. You can't make a sound. I know it hurts, but you can't imagine what they'll do to you if they catch us. I'm going to get you out of here, Jones. I'm going to get you back to your family but you have to be quiet."

His hand slowly came up, about to cover her mouth. She couldn't be sure what would happen next, but she knew she had a shot at changing the script playing out in his head. She was betting Jones wasn't female.

She brought her mouth to his, catching him in a kiss.

His head immediately came up, his eyes flaring. "What the hell?" He stared down at her, obviously back to his normal, taciturn self. "Karina? What are you doing?"

She bit back a giggle because she wasn't sure how he thought she'd managed to get underneath him to "do" something. "Welcome back to the real world, Brighton. That was a hell of a dream you were having."

He shook his head and finally managed to roll off her. "I was dreaming about something that happened a while back." He shoved a hand across his hair. "Did I hurt you?"

Karina moved toward him. It was instinctive, she told herself. She comforted people and Derek was obviously in need. It had nothing to do with how much she wanted to put her hands on him again, how much she longed to be close to him. "You didn't hurt me, Derek. I'm fine."

She placed a hand on his shoulder, but he was on his feet in an instant, looking down on her, his eyes narrowed. "You're just lucky. You can't be anywhere near me when I get into that state. I could have hurt you. You have no fucking idea what goes through my head."

Oh, she'd heard enough, knew enough about his history to guess. "You were going to put your hand across my mouth to keep me quiet, Brighton. It wasn't exactly a vicious attack."

His jaw hardened, every word coming out of his mouth in a harsh grind. "So you thought it would be a good idea to try to get some? What the fuck was that, Karina? If you want a little cock, all you have to do is ask. I already told you I'm more than willing to fuck you while we're on the case. But I don't like being manipulated."

Oh, she was done with him. "You know what, Brighton? Screw you. The next time I hear you crying out in the middle of the night, I'll ignore it and let you stay wherever the hell it is you go. I was trying to help you."

"By having sex with me? You really know how to help a guy."

He was an ass. She got off the floor and got into his space. He needed to understand that he couldn't intimidate her. "Well, I had two choices in how to deal with you. I could kiss you and hope that brought you out of it because I'm betting Jones wasn't someone you would exchange saliva with, or I could have brought my knee up and made sure you could taste your own semen. I know which one I'll pick next time."

She turned to go, but he gripped her wrist. "I'm not done."

With two sharp twists, she was out of his hold. "I am. Good night, Brighton. Sweet dreams."

She slammed the door between them and immediately the tears started. She turned and put her back to the door, sliding down. There was zero point in getting back in bed. She wouldn't sleep.

He was such a bastard. Screw him. She didn't need him. She was perfectly fine on her own. She would keep the door closed between them and in the morning they would go right back to being somewhat chilly strangers. That was the only way to deal with him.

She would ignore the heat between them because he couldn't possibly feel it. If he felt it, he would be kinder, want more from her. He wouldn't bat her away like a wounded bear.

"It was Afghanistan." His voice was quiet, but she could easily hear him through the door. She felt it the minute he put his back to the door on his side.

She didn't care. Not a bit. Nope. She didn't give a shit that he'd been in Afghanistan and served his country and apparently still had nightmares about it. "Did you get pinned down?"

Yes, she was just a little curious. No more than that.

There was a long sigh from the other side of the door. "Yeah. We were close-quarters fighting. We got into a firefight in Fallujah and me and Jones got cut off from the rest of the team. You got to understand. The streets are really narrow and when your adrenaline is up, you just kind of react. It was a part of the city we hadn't been in before. Taliban held."

"So you were surrounded?"

"Not exactly. It was just the two of us and he'd taken some fire. I had to get him out of there. I thought I remembered the way back, but I just took us deeper in."

She closed her eyes, not wanting to think about how horrifying that must have been. On the run without the rest of his team, Brighton would have felt a deep sense of responsibility for Jones. "How bad off was your teammate?"

"He'd taken a couple to his right leg. By the time we could stop, he was bleeding pretty freely. I found an abandoned building and we slipped inside. It was rat infested, a real pit, but I didn't have another option. I had to stop the bleeding."

"And keep him quiet. He was probably in a lot of pain," she guessed.

"Yes. I had to put him in worse pain because I had to dig the bullet out. He screamed. God, I can still hear it and I couldn't do anything but stuff a rag in his mouth because they were everywhere. I could hear them moving around, shouting at others to look for us. They actually came in at one point. I hid us under some garbage. I kept my hand over his mouth so he couldn't cry out. I damn near suffocated him. Do you know what I felt like in that moment?"

Powerless. He would have been utterly out of control and praying to anyone who would listen to save him. How humbling must that have been for a man like Derek? She couldn't help it. She was stupid. Utterly ridiculous. She knew it was dumb, but she softened toward him. Her heart was an ignorant thing. It just kept reaching out.

"How did you get out?"

There was a long moment where she worried she'd lost him. He would go back to his couch and she to her bed, both in their respective corners, and the fight would begin again in the morning like nothing had happened the night before.

"He bled out." The words sounded hollow, utterly haunted. "I tried to tie the damage off. I tried to stay up so I could watch over him. But I fucking fell asleep and when I woke up he was dead. He was twenty-three years old. I'd promised to get him back to his family."

"I'm going to open the door now." She couldn't just sit there when he obviously needed affection.

She heard him shuffling, moving even as she opened the door. And then he was there, his muscular body seeming to shrink in on itself.

"You can't be around me when I'm like that, Karina. I could have hurt you."

She followed her instincts now and walked right up to him. He didn't move as she folded her arms around him, tucking her head under his chin. "I wasn't going to let you hurt me, Derek. I had a plan."

It took him a couple of seconds, but his arms wrapped around her, squeezing her tight. His big palm came over her head in a protective gesture that warmed her. "What was your plan?"

It felt so good to be in his arms. The man knew how to hug. He enveloped her, surrounded her. She couldn't help but cuddle closer. "I kissed you because I figured the dream was from your Army days. I'd tried to talk you awake, but I figured you probably hadn't kissed your Army buddy a whole lot."

He chuckled and she felt it all along her spine. "No. I hadn't even kissed Jones once. It was effective. You stayed calm, didn't you? I didn't really worry you at all."

She would bet he'd freaked the hell out of other women. "It takes a lot to panic me, Brighton. I know you don't like it, but I can handle myself. And I can handle you. You weren't going to hurt me."

"I almost killed Maia once. I thought I was trying to keep Jones quiet, but she was smaller than him. I covered her nose, too. She couldn't breathe. She hit me, but I didn't wake up. She finally managed to pick up a glass on the nightstand and broke it over my thick skull."

So he had his reasons to be worried. "I'm not Maia. I'm bigger and stronger than she is. I bet she hasn't had the same self-defense training I've had."

His hands began to stroke her. One flowed over her hair, the other down her back. "Yeah, she wouldn't have thought to kiss me. Do you think you might want to kiss me in some situation other than trying to save your own life?"

Such a drama queen. She lifted her head and found him staring down at her. Heart-stoppingly sexy. That's what he was. With his sleepy eyes and that sexy beard of his, she couldn't quite look away from him. And his lips. Oh, they were plump and sensual and she wondered what it would feel like to have those lips on her body, worshiping her skin, kissing and licking and sucking.

She had a choice. She could step back and go to her widow's bed or she could make one small move and the night wouldn't be spent alone. She would spend it in his arms and she would finally know what it felt like to be Derek Brighton's woman—even if only for a little while.

With a shaky breath, she went on her toes and pressed her lips to his.

* * * *

Derek's whole body reacted to her. His heart pounded, his skin tingled. Every available ounce of blood seemed to flow right to his dick. She was saying yes. She was offering herself, and he wasn't about to turn her down.

The need to burn off the dream was riding him hard. When he'd finally woken up and found Karina's body trapped under his, he'd damn near lost it. He could have hurt her, could have killed her. It was precisely why he didn't sleep with women. He fucked and pleasured and found his comfort in their bodies, but he went to his own bed so he couldn't hurt them.

Except Karina really did seem to have handled him.

He gave her a minute, allowed her to explore. Her mouth was oddly tentative for an experienced woman, but then Karina seemed to be a study in contradictions. She was on her toes, her hands moving from around his chest to his jawline where she brushed against his beard, her light touches making him shiver slightly.

He didn't shiver. He didn't get this weird tightness in his stomach. He fucked. He brought pleasure. He didn't get worried or nervous.

But he was kind of both because he wanted her so fucking bad, he couldn't see straight.

From the moment he'd woken up and found her underneath him, his cock had jumped and pleaded and twitched in his pants. His brain might know that she wasn't his type but his cock had entirely different ideas about what was attractive.

She kissed him and he kept still, allowing her to explore, to be in charge for now because she wouldn't be later. What was attractive? She was. God, he loved the fact that she'd been willing to take off his balls if she had to. He also kind of loved that she'd come up with a way to save his balls.

He could still remember Maia crying. She'd sobbed for hours after the incident. Not Karina. Karina had that crazy sexy smile on her face that let him know she hadn't been bothered at all by his PTSD dreams. She'd handled it. She'd taken care of it and she hadn't needed to nearly kill him to do it.

Karina wasn't his forever sub, but damn he wanted her now.

She stopped, pulling slightly back. When she looked up at him, he nearly got to his knees.

She was fucking gorgeous. She bit her bottom lip, obviously nervous. "Do you want me to stop?"

He had zero plans to stop. He might never fucking stop. A dangerous thought played through his head. He didn't have to stop. He could fuck Karina until he didn't have an ounce of come in his body and then he'd just wait until he had more and he'd give that to her, too.

"Yes. I want you to stop." Because it was far past time for him to take over.

Her face fell, the sweetest pink flushing through her. He loved her skin when she was embarrassed or emotional. She couldn't hide from him. It all played out over that precious flesh of hers. "Okay."

She started to take a step away, but he wouldn't allow it. She might be able to handle him when he was asleep, but he was going to make it very plain that he was her Master when he was awake. He caught her, pulling her to his body, letting her feel every ounce of his will because it was all directed her way.

"I want you to stop because I'm the top, Karina." He practically growled at her. He'd never wanted to dominate a woman as much as he wanted to dominate Karina. He wanted to bend her to his will, to watch her give in to him because she was the fucking alpha female and that meant she belonged to him. She wouldn't submit to anyone else—man or woman. Only to him because he was strong. She was everything he needed her to be.

She gasped a little, the action bringing her breasts in close contact with his chest. Her nipples had peaked, her eyes softening. Even the hands on his body had become something different. Before, she'd held him, but the minute he asserted dominance they became cajoling, pleading for his affection, his praise.

Submission. She offered him the sweetest submission of all. The submission of an alpha female to her chosen top. She would never get on her knees for another man. She wouldn't allow a lesser the access to her body, the opening to her soul. Only him. In a haze of lust, he fucking believed all of it. He believed it was true. He no longer gave a damn about the dream. Reality was far better. Reality was Karina submitting to him, giving him everything he wanted.

He dragged her against his body, pressing his pelvis to her, letting her feel just how much he wanted her. He wanted to burn away that dream in the hot depths of her body. Karina could handle it. Karina could take his rough impulses. She might even fucking like them.

"Give over to me," he whispered against her lips. "Give me everything you have. Let me in."

Into more than just her pussy. In that moment, he wanted to drive into her, to make a place for himself there, a home that he never had to leave.

He hauled her up, lifting her like she weighed nothing. He pulled her against his chest, gripping her ass so she had nowhere to go. Her legs dangled for half a second before coming around his waist. It was one easy move to shift and shove her against the wall of her bedroom, grinding down on her clit. That was her sweet spot. She moaned and groaned when he pushed on that little jewel. What the hell would she do when he sucked on it?

He pressed her against the wall, his pelvis hard on hers. So fucking good. He wanted to drown in her.

Her legs wound around his waist. It would be easy, so easy, to push that little T-shirt she was wearing up. He could drag her panties down and let his cock free. He didn't want easy. He wanted long and hard. He wanted it to last all fucking night.

He wanted to never think about anything but Karina again.

He pressed against her, lighting his whole body up. He kissed her, dominating her the way he'd always wanted to. His mouth pushed against hers, pressing in and taking control. She submitted, sweetly flowering open for his tongue. He took advantage, dancing against hers in a silky glide, so relieved when her tongue moved, joining him.

She was open and willing. She filled him with joy, with fucking happiness, because he'd never had a woman like her. Need rose hard and fast—the need to slip a collar around her throat so she couldn't run when she realized he wasn't worth it.

He kissed her hard and long. So warm. So sweet. So fucking gorgeous.

He needed to be inside her, needed to taste her on his tongue. Needed to know he'd given her crazy pleasure. He walked the two steps it took to get to her bed and tossed her gently down. She landed on her back, and he could see how her nipples poked against the fabric of her shirt.

"Spread your legs for me." He needed her to want him. Needed her to spread herself for his pleasure.

She didn't hesitate. He'd expected her to, had almost expected her to argue, but she simply moved her legs farther apart. She simply opened herself to him, giving him access to all her sweet spots.

Fuck. She wasn't wearing panties. Her pussy was right there, spread wide for him to see and she was already wet. His cock was so damn hard, but he wasn't going to give in yet. The fucker had waited this long, it could wait a little longer. He needed to prove something to her, to himself. He needed to prove to her that he had some semblance of control and he needed to prove to himself that she wasn't going to taste as good as he thought she would. She couldn't possibly.

He dropped to his knees, grasping her ankles and dragging her to the edge of the bed. Silky smooth skin caressed his fingertips and he could smell her. He breathed it in, reveling in the scent of her arousal. The petals of her sex were already coated, her labia a gorgeous coral shade.

"You want me."

"I know I shouldn't," she whispered back.

He couldn't think of all the reasons why this was a bad idea. Right now it seemed like the best fucking thing that had ever happened to him. With the exception of his career, he'd rambled through life ever since coming home from the war. He'd taken the pleasures he'd been offered, but he hadn't wanted, really wanted anything until he'd seen Karina. It might not last, but he would take it. He would take this passion and enjoy it because he felt alive for the first time in forever.

And hungry. So fucking hungry for her.

"I'll make you forget. All the reasons this is a bad idea—you won't remember them when I'm done with you." With shaky hands, he touched her, sliding his fingers through the soft skin of her sex. He ran the pad of his thumb over her clitoris and she jumped. Karina moaned and pressed up against him, trying to force him to rub her harder.

Pure pleasure coursed through him because she was going to make this so much sweeter for him. He flipped her over and immediately laid a quick two smacks to that gorgeous ass.

She whimpered, an entirely sexy sound. "I'm so sorry. I didn't...It's been a long time, Sir."

Did she think being polite would make him go easy on her? Sweet little brat. "Who's in charge, Karina?"

"You are, Sir." Her answer came out in a breathy huff that made his cock jump.

He would prefer Master, but he hadn't come close to earning that yet. "I am. I'm in charge of this. I'm in charge of your pleasure. I'll give it to you, but you have to trust me." He leaned over and kissed the places he'd just smacked. "I'm going to turn you back over and you're going to be still for me. Do I need to tie you down?"

"No. I'll stay still. I'll be good."

"I will tie you down, Karina. Eventually I'm going to truss you up like the pretty bird you are and I'll have you any way I want you. But I want you to obey me on your own tonight." What he didn't say was why. He didn't want to tie her down tonight because he wanted her arms around him, her legs squeezing him tight when he entered her. He flipped her back over, confident she would obey. "Be good or the next time it's going to be twenty and I'll make you count it out. Neither one of us wants that."

He saw something he did want though. The girl liked to be spanked. Their kinks dovetailed nicely since he'd never enjoyed spanking an ass as much as he did Karina's. Her pussy was glistening in the low light. He couldn't tease her another moment more. He leaned over and ran his tongue over her labia.

She tasted far better than he'd imagined. Sweet and spicy, she coated his tongue and he couldn't get enough of her. She tensed beneath him as he held her legs open. Her soft gasps and long sighs played along with the desperate tension in her thighs. She was being so good when it was obvious to him that she wanted to move, wanted to force him to go deeper.

"Do you need something, gorgeous?"

"Derek, please. Please, I'm so close. It's been so long since I felt like this."

He wanted to be the best she'd ever had. He wanted her to remember him long after they were no longer together. It was perverse, but he wanted to be the man she thought about the rest of her life. "You want to come? Ask me politely."

He rubbed her clit just enough to make her squirm but not enough to send her over the edge.

"Please, Sir. I need it so much. Please let me come." The words were so stinking sweet coming out of her mouth. She usually cursed his very name, but having Karina Mills begging him did amazing things for his ego. He could turn his spitting cat into a sweet little kitten and all he had to do was put his hands and mouth on her. It was that simple. She responded to him like no woman ever had before. So quick. So pure. So fucking honest.

And she'd been polite so she should be rewarded.

He let himself off the leash. He fucked her with his tongue, diving deep inside and glorying in the way she shook around him. Through his haze of lust he could hear her crying out even while she obeyed him and remained as still as she could. His thumb found her clit and he pressed down as he speared her with his tongue.

She came with a little moan and his tongue was coated with her.

He couldn't wait another fucking second. He had to have her. He'd done his job. He'd made her come and now she was his for the night. He stood up and dropped his PJ pants to the floor after palming the condom he'd put in his pocket. "Give me the T-shirt."

He wanted her naked, nothing between them except that crappy but necessary piece of latex. He was a bastard, but he was prepared. He'd slipped one into his PJ bottoms earlier when she'd sat next to him on the couch. Nothing had come from that, but he was damn happy to have it now.

He stroked himself, once and again while watching her. He would love to have her roll the condom on with her mouth, but he was far too impatient. In one practiced move, he slid the condom on.

Karina seemed to be coming out of her submissive state. She bit her bottom lip as she stared up at him.

No. That was so not going to happen. He wasn't about to let her get away. He leaned over and kissed her again. "You taste so good, gorgeous." He licked along her bottom lip. "Taste yourself. You're all over my tongue. Stay with me."

Her arms were around him again. She opened her mouth and let him in. Over and over he stroked her with his tongue, the intimacy unfamiliar but sweet. He rarely kissed anymore. Sex had become an exchange of need. How long had it been since he'd had to have it? Since he couldn't take another breath without thinking about being inside a woman. Karina. Only Karina.

"Let me in, gorgeous. Let me inside. I fucking need you tonight." He wasn't sure he could walk away. He might do something horrible. He might actually beg.

She pulled the shirt off, exposing her lovely breasts.

It was all the invitation he needed. He fell on her like a starving man. Soft. She was so soft. He gave her his weight because while she was soft, she was strong, too. Karina could handle him. He could fuck her as hard as he wanted and she would take it.

He started to spread her legs, to shove himself in, and then he saw her.

She might have just had an orgasm, but she wasn't ready for him yet. She was holding on to him, but there was fear in her eyes. God, he didn't want to see that.

But he wasn't willing to let her go. Kissing. She liked to be kissed. He covered her mouth with his, gently this time. "Stay with me, gorgeous."

"It's been a while. I…I'm nervous."

"I'll take care of you." He was going to make sure she came again, make sure she had every bit of pleasure he could give her.

He leaned over to kiss her and prayed he could make her want him again.

# Chapter Six

It was the sight of the condom that did it. Karina took a deep breath and realized this was really happening. She was about to open herself and let Derek Brighton in. She hadn't had sex in years, hadn't even wanted to share that with someone else.

He'd promised to take care of her, but she was sure he meant that in a sexual way. He couldn't possibly mean anything else and she couldn't expect more.

But suddenly she wanted to. She wanted this to be real. If only for a night.

"I can take care of myself, Brighton." She wasn't going to dive into maudlin thoughts. Five years had gone by and if she never moved on, she would regret it. She'd loved Kevin, but he was gone. And Liam was right. He would have wanted her to be happy. Could she ever be happy with Brighton? Would she hate herself if she didn't try?

He'd said she wasn't his type and she'd given him those words right back, but the minute he touched her, she'd gone up in flames. She'd never wanted a man the way she wanted him.

He gave her the craziest, sexiest grin. "I'm sure you can, gorgeous, but you don't have to take care of yourself tonight. Let me take care of you."

He lowered himself down again and Karina couldn't help but welcome him. She didn't even want to think about all the ways this could go wrong. She just wanted him.

It was time to stop thinking and let herself feel for once. Yes, she would likely get her heart ripped in two, but at least she would feel something beyond the numbness of the last several years.

"I want to make you feel good, gorgeous. Let me make you feel so good." He whispered the words against her skin. She felt the rumble of his voice all along her flesh.

Heat poured through her body, the thrum of arousal a rhythm

she couldn't deny. She could still feel his tongue on her tenderest flesh. He hadn't played around. He'd eaten her like she was the sweetest peach. What would he say if she told him the truth? What would he say if she told him she'd never been kissed there? That he was the first man to lick her and suck her and make her want to scream because she couldn't take another second of his sweet torture.

Making love with Kevin had been wonderful, but Derek made her feel things she'd never imagined. Even his weight did something for her. He was so much bigger than her husband had been. He pressed her into the mattress, his legs spreading hers and making a place for himself. His chest came down on hers, the light hair there rasping against her nipples.

"God, you're so fucking beautiful, Karina." His lips hovered above hers. "I want you so badly. Tell me I can have you."

He was right there, his hips pumping against her. His cock was pressed to her clit and the heat was building all over again. Sweet want coursed through her. She let her hands find his hair. How was it so soft?

"Please, Sir." She loved using that word on him. He was so dominant, so strong and yet he'd done something Kevin never had. Kevin never slipped out of his Dom role when they made love. He never gave up a second of control. He'd told her he needed it and she'd believed him, but there was something about Derek's softness that made her melt. Kevin would never have asked her. He would have assumed if she didn't use her safe word that everything was fine.

She'd never heard a man practically begging, needing her the way Derek seemed to tonight.

She couldn't resist. She opened herself because she didn't know how to do this any other way. She wrapped herself around him, offering him everything she had.

"You won't regret it, gorgeous." His mouth fused to hers, his tongue cajoling as he fitted his cock against her pussy and started to press inside.

She held on. He was so big. She gasped, but he'd done a damn good job of getting her ridiculously wet. He slid in an inch or so and held himself still, his forehead against hers.

"You're going to kill me, Karina. Naturally you feel this good. Fuck, you're so tight." He pulled back a little and then carefully moved forward. His mouth came back on hers and he captured the little cry she made as he pressed his full length inside.

So full. Derek seemed to take up all the space, his cock foraging deep. She held on to him.

"Yes, you dig those nails in. I want it. You won't hurt me." He pulled out and fucked back in, keeping his strokes measured, grinding his pelvis against hers. Every motion was careful, but she could see the toll it was taking on him. His face was flushed and tense.

She stroked his back, letting her hands go down to cup that wretchedly hot backside of his. "Give me more, Sir. Please."

She wanted all of him. She wanted for him to lose control the way she was. Yes, she loved to play, loved to be controlled by her Dom, but she needed this, too. She needed to feel precious, sexy and wanted.

"I'll give you everything." He leveraged himself up on his arms and slammed against her pelvis, giving her the hard length of his dick in one thrust.

Karina felt him grind down on her even as he stroked that place deep inside that made her go off like a rocket. She didn't fight it. She let that orgasm explode across her body. Wave after wave of pleasure sparked through her. She held on to Derek even as he lost that controlled rhythm he'd used and began to fuck her with pure force. His hands tightened on her, holding on as he slammed into her again and again. His eyes closed and his head dropped back and then he shouted out her name as he held himself hard against her.

Even as he came, she felt the sparks again, the aftershocks of the earthquake he'd started deep in her body.

He collapsed down, his face next to hers, his body warm against her own.

Blood thrummed through her system, pulsing in the most pleasant way. She sighed and let the softness of the moment settle on her.

She half expected him to jump off the moment he was done, but Derek cuddled down, settling his head on her chest.

She let her hands brush through his hair. "How did you get away? Back in Afghanistan, I mean."

He hadn't finished his story and she found herself so curious. He rolled off her, but immediately settled at her side again. He propped his head up on his hand and stared at her for a moment. "Big Tag came after me. He went against orders and he found me." He brought his free hand out to run his thumb over her lip. "It was the morning after Jones died. If I'd been able to keep him alive just another couple of hours…"

She shook her head. "You did everything you could."

"Sometimes I wonder about that. Karina, I should go and sleep on the couch, but I don't want to."

Dangerous. If she thought he was dangerous before, this Derek just might kill her. She'd expected him to get up and stretch and walk out. She'd thought he might kiss her and thank her for the lay. Not once in any scenario that played through her head had he put his head to her breast and asked for her comfort.

"Please stay with me." She was in too deep, but she couldn't get out. Not now.

"I don't want to hurt you."

She was pretty sure he wasn't talking just about the physical. She was rapidly discovering that Derek wanted to play fair. He wanted to be honest. "Just stay with me for a while."

"I don't sleep with other people, Karina. I can't. So I'll just lay here until you fall asleep. If you wake up and I'm not here, don't take it bad. I'm just not built that way anymore, okay?"

She could handle honesty. "All right."

She let her fingers rub his scalp and despite all of his protests, his chest rose and fell in an even rhythm and he was asleep within moments.

Karina smiled as she managed to turn off the light.

She held him and couldn't help but think that no matter what happened, they wouldn't be the same. A new life. She'd just started over.

Though it made her ache inside, she didn't even regret it. She kissed the top of Derek's head and let herself drift off to sleep.

* * * *

Early morning light filtered in through the slats and Karina sighed a little as she turned.

And then remembered what had happened the night before.

She let her eyes fly open, but she was alone in bed. The pillow next to her still had an indention where his head had rested. She'd woken up once in the night to find him wrapped around her, his arm anchored around her middle, his body spooning hers.

Who would have guessed that big bad Derek Brighton was a teddy bear?

Okay. So she'd slept with him. That didn't really change anything between them. It didn't make them best buddies. It didn't even really mean they were friends. It meant they had needed each other in the middle of the night and they were consenting adults without significant others.

She could handle this. Sure she hadn't actually dated in over fifteen years, but then they weren't dating. They were...what were they? Intimate strangers? Fuck buddies? When this case was over would he call her up when he needed a lay? Would she shove the phone up his ass? Or would she get used to casual sex?

It hadn't felt casual.

It had felt real. It felt oddly pure to be with Brighton, like something she'd been missing for a long time had finally fallen into place.

She was acting like a kid. He would likely run if he knew that thought was going through her head.

"You need a maid."

She nearly jumped and pulled the sheet up, covering her breasts. Where had she put the shirt she'd been wearing the night before? Derek stood in her doorway wearing nothing but a towel wrapped around his lean hips. His hair was slightly wet, and even from where she was she could smell the fresh scent of soap clinging to his every muscle. And there were so many of them. So many gorgeous muscles. She hadn't taken the time to properly look at him last night. She'd seen him without his shirt before, but somehow it was different without the encasement of his leathers. From the golden tan of his skin to the way his abs flowed into sexy notches on his hips, he was sin on two legs. Even his scars seemed beautiful to her.

And she was supposed to be an adult female who had merely had a fun night with an equally adult male.

"I've been busy lately. I'll try to clean up this morning." Casual. Cool. She wasn't bothered at all by the fact that she was lying around naked. Nope. Not at all.

He chuckled a little and leaned against the doorjamb. "Come on, Mills. You got to be able to take a joke."

"It's not really a joke. I think I saw something growing in the fridge. I haven't been very attentive to housekeeping lately." She bet any girlfriend of Derek's likely was. He seemed to be an organized guy. His desk was always neat as a pin. She was lucky if she could find anything on hers.

"Yeah, pretty sure that was going to rise up and take us all down one of these days. Luckily I think I tossed it out before it gained intelligence and led a fungal revolution."

She felt her cheeks flare. "God, Brighton, you didn't have to do that."

"I did if I'm going to keep my sanity. I'm the slightest bit OCD about some things, including being able to open the fridge with little to no fear that I'll be attacked. The good news is now it's clean and I'm going to show you something amazing. It's called food. You see, we buy these things like eggs and milk and then they're waiting there when we want to cook."

She couldn't help but send him her middle finger. Something about the man brought out the worst in her. "I cooked last night."

"And you only bought the stuff for dinner."

"Which you ate all of. Normally that would last me a week."

"Now you have to feed me," he said, his voice dropping. "And I like to eat, Karina. I'm a big guy and I need a lot to satisfy me. How about we make a deal? We're stuck together for a while. I'll clean. You cook. If you do breakfast anything like you did dinner, I will happily dust this whole place."

Somehow the idea of Derek walking around with a duster in his hand made her giggle. "I had no idea how handy you were. I kind of thought you would have some sub do that for you. Aren't you looking for a slave?"

His smile faltered. "Yes, well we know that's nothing you're interested in. If we're going to survive this I have to be a little less rigid. Besides, I guess I never really thought about that part. I wasn't trying to find a maid. I've cleaned up after myself for a long time."

Then what exactly was he expecting his chosen sub to do all day if she wasn't keeping house? It wasn't forever, but he was right. They needed some rules if they were going to share her very small space. She just needed to be able to get her eyes off his chest long enough to think about what a good rule would be. Maybe he shouldn't walk around shirtless so she didn't turn into a drooling idiot every time he entered the room.

"What do you say?" Derek asked. "I'll even put together that bookshelf you shoved into the front closet."

She groaned a little. "All the instructions are in Swedish. I'm not very handy."

"I am. I think you'll find me very handy to have around. Do we have a deal?"

He must be really hungry. "Yes. Now if you give me a sec, I'll shower and get breakfast going."

"We have plenty of time. Now for the second part of our deal. Drop the sheet. I want to see you."

"What?"

"I want to see your breasts. I want to see your legs. Hell, I want to see your toes, gorgeous. I want to see the way your skin looks in the morning light because I dreamed about it all last night. That's right. My dreams are usually shitty, but last night I dreamed about fucking you and I slept like a baby. So drop the sheet and show me."

Last night seemed like a dream. "Derek, I don't know if that's a good idea."

"Just play with me. Sleep with me. Be with me for a week, maybe two. Think of it as a vacation from where you usually are. I don't know about you, but I'm lonely. I would really like to take a vacation from being alone even if it's just for a little while. Hell, I'll be honest. I want you more than I want my next breath. I just...can't we just be for a while?"

If he'd pushed her, if he'd talked about fucking or screwing around or even called it sex, she might have been able to get up and walk away. His words had begun an ache that pierced through her because she hadn't really known how lonely she'd been until he'd kissed her. He might be using her as a stand-in for his perfect submissive, but she knew that the only reason he could fill the void was because he was Derek.

Karina let the sheet drop.

"Lie back. Spread your legs for me. I know you're going to cook, but I'm hungry now. I'm so fucking hungry for you." He dropped his towel and crawled on the bed.

Karina laid back, her eyes closing as he did exactly what he'd promised and ate his fill.

# Chapter Seven

Derek looked out over the club and thanked the universe he'd met Ian Taggart. Not just for the fact that the son of a bitch was loyal as fuck and had saved his life but also because the dude hired a cleaning staff. Sanctum was always clean.

He was pretty sure there were no maids on call at Kink. The place had a distinctly industrial feel crossed with what he believed a back alley looked like after the trash truck crashed and burned.

"Are you okay, hon?" Karina put a hand on his back.

She was the prettiest thing in the room with her emerald green corset setting off her gorgeous skin. And she smelled clean. God, he really liked clean. He put an arm around her waist and brought her close, breathing in the smell of her shampoo. Two days into sleeping with her and the scent of lavender got him hard every time he caught a whiff.

"I'm fine. Tell me about the people you've met here."

She seemed to already know everyone. From what he understood, she'd been coming here for only a couple of weeks. The way she explained it, she'd started visiting the club as part of a case. She'd been hired by the mother of the second victim. He'd met her when he'd followed Karina around for a day. He'd been surprised at her office. It was small and cheap. Her clients had been a revelation as well. He'd expected her to work for corporate types but it seemed she mostly focused her attention on the underprivileged. In addition to taking two cases he was pretty sure she wouldn't be paid for, she found a couple of homeless men shelter and managed to scare the shit out of a guy who'd been stalking his ex-wife and kid.

Yeah, he'd gotten a hard-on watching her do that, too.

She came in close, brushing her chest against his. "The woman in the back is called Starr, not her real name. Her Dom is Master Will. He's actually quite reasonable. From what I've uncovered, she's a receptionist and he's an EMT with the city. I'm pretty sure she's cheating on him with the guy behind the bar."

He glanced at the bartender. He was wearing leathers, but Derek would bet they were strictly for show. "Why do you think that?"

The faintest hint of a smile crossed her lips. "Mostly because I caught them fucking in the bathroom."

Derek frowned. "Well, if it's anything like the rest of the place, they probably have Ebola now."

The slight grin went crazy, sexy brilliant. God, he loved it when she smiled his way. "You would think that, Monk."

She liked to tease him about his very normal and hygienic need to be bacteria free. "I will continue to think that and I will also use my personal kit. Did I see a wall of public toys? Because that made me a little sick."

"This is one of those places that went up pretty much overnight. It's a tourist place, which is why I was surprised to meet Master Will. There are a couple of well-meaning people, but most of them are strictly tourists. I've even caught a couple of gawkers but as long as they pay the fee, the management doesn't seem to care. This place only says it's private to get around a couple of laws. They pretty much accept anyone who can afford it."

Unlike Sanctum. Big Tag carefully controlled the Doms and subs he allowed access to Sanctum. Most clubs came about as very private play places for friends. From what Derek could tell, most of these people didn't know each other. It was a dangerous way to play. "What kind of security do they have?"

"Well, now they have Li," Karina offered.

He felt his blood pressure tick up. "No security. No real dungeon monitors from what I can tell." He saw her start to perk up but shut that shit down quickly. "No. Liam doesn't count. He just started. Was there a dungeon monitor while you were working here alone?"

Her nose scrunched up. "There was this one guy named Matt, but he apparently only showed up when he was sober. You'll find they also don't have a two-drink maximum."

She was killing him. "I don't want to know what you've had to put up with, do I?"

The little shrug she gave him didn't up his confidence in her ability to make smart choices. "I handled it."

He was just about to launch into a lecture about how she would "handle" things from now on. He'd been perfecting his list of rules which absolutely included never ever being in a club like this alone again and walking around in a thong among drunk assholes. It would happen over his dead body. Unfortunately, Master Will took that moment to catch sight of Karina, and he took his sub's hand and made a beeline for them. He caught sight of Starr.

On the surface she was everything he loved about women. Not a hair out of place. She was dressed in an angelic white corset and a tiny thong that showed off a set of legs that seemed to go on for miles. She was perfectly tanned, her breasts a nice size and likely extremely firm because he was pretty sure they were like the rest of Starr—utterly fake.

She showed no expression as her Master led her along. She simply obeyed and when Master Will stopped in front of them, she sank with perfection to her knees beside him, her eyes cast down.

Perfect nails. Perfect body. Perfect submission.

Why did she leave him cold?

"Karina, have you heard the news?" Master Will's eyes had softened, his voice going low as though he handled all the subs with the most delicate of hands.

Karina stopped and he could tell from the sudden flush of her skin that she'd gotten emotional. About Amanda. He wasn't sure what she'd told anyone about her connection to Amanda so he kept his mouth shut, merely standing behind her and placing his hands on her shoulder in a show of support—and a caveman-like "girl is mine" gesture. Yeah, that was in there, too. Master Will looked to be in his early thirties, fit, and not unattractive. Hell, the subs at Sanctum would likely be all over the guy. But Karina wasn't going to be.

"News?" While her skin had flushed slightly, her voice was cool and composed.

Yes, she could definitely handle herself and he wasn't going to play poker with her anytime soon.

"Sweetheart, you need to watch yourself. I think someone's working the club circuit. According to some of my cop friends, there have been several females killed in the last couple of months who attended clubs like this one." The big Dom put a hand on his sub's head as though trying to comfort her. As far as Derek could tell, Starr didn't need comfort. Her expression never changed. She simply stared down at the floor. "I've talked to some of the Doms here and we want to institute new rules. The management here sucks and we all know it so the new bartender and I decided we should make sure the subs all have an escort into and out of the club, and then you should have a Dom you can call when you make it home all right."

Sean was the new bartender, and he'd just instituted one of Sanctum's most rigidly followed rules.

He didn't even like to think about what happened if a sub didn't follow the rules at Sanctum. That would not be an erotic spanking. Despite Sean's best intentions, it might be harder to implement here.

O'Donnell and the Brit split duties escorting Karina when she was playing at Sanctum. What would it feel like when their contract was done and he wasn't the guy taking care of her?

"That sounds like a good idea." There was a smile in her voice. She would be encouraging the poor kid. Who hadn't thought of a couple of problems with the scenario.

"How well do you know the other Doms?" Derek asked.

Will frowned. "They seem like great guys."

Amateur. "So did Ted Bundy. As for that, I don't actually know you so I don't think I'll have you escorting anyone. How do I know this isn't a ploy to get a sub alone? The parking lot out there doesn't even have security lights. You could get a sub in the dark and do what you like with her and all in the name of protecting her."

Will's shoulders squared. "Who the fuck are you?"

"I'm Karina's Dom."

"I thought you said you didn't have a Dom."

"She lied."

Karina shot him a look that could have peeled paint off the walls. If they had thought to actually paint the walls anyway. She turned back to Will with a gracious smile. "He's my ex. My current. Gosh, I don't even know how to classify us half the time. We're one of those crazy on-again, off-again couples who can break up faster than we made up."

Yep, there was a warning in there that didn't actually scare him in the slightest. She could get as pissed as she liked. He knew what made her melt. He touched the nape of her neck, just a tiny reminder, and sure enough she shivered a little. "We're on again and it's going to stay that way. I'm Derek."

"You a cop?" Will asked, his eyes narrowing.

It was interesting that he went there, though Derek had to admit EMTs worked with a lot of cops. EMTs, firefighters, cops, they were a little community and it wasn't surprising that an EMT could peg him as a cop. "I used to be. I work for private security now. Got tired of getting my ass shot at for nothing."

A hint of the truth was always the way to go.

"You know what they say." Karina seemed to be doing her level best to smooth things over. "Once a cop, always a cop. One day he'll learn some manners."

"That's twenty." It used to annoy the hell out of him when she would turn that sassy mouth his way. She had a sharp tongue, but she also had a great ass that he loved to spank. When she got bratty, he got spanky. Everything worked out. "And shouldn't you allow Master Will and I to work out our differences? Perhaps he would respect our relationship more if you were in a proper submissive position."

She didn't try to have a poker face with him. She sent him a fierce frown, her voice tight. "Of course, Master."

She sank to her knees beside him. Yes, he was going to pay for that later. Oddly, he was looking forward to it. Now that they had a contract in place, it was easier for him to relax around her. They had banged it out in bed in between...well, banging. He couldn't stop the grin that crossed his face when he remembered going over her hard and soft limits and how she'd hit him with a pillow when he tried to get her to agree that figging was an appropriate punishment for backtalk.

She hadn't agreed, but damn he wanted to watch her squirm.

He looked back at Master Will and decided it was time to put aside his bad cop routine and go on a charm offensive. He could be charming. Maybe. "Look, man, I'm sorry to come off paranoid but I just got back into town and found out this one has been playing some dangerous games. I don't think going to clubs on her own was very smart and I think it even less now that I know subs are being killed. Do you know how many?"

He wanted to watch Will as he talked about the killings. Some killers loved to brag. Some just wanted to be a part of the drama. He could tell a lot by how the other man reacted.

Will turned serious, dropping any act. His hand stayed in his sub's hair, still giving comfort where it looked like none was needed. Was the poor dude completely clueless about his lady or was this all a little play? "As far as I can tell, it's at least three subs, all women. I don't know if they're related, but it seems a little coincidental. Two of them had come to this club, but they were about as different as they could be. Tanya was sweet. She was just a kid looking for someone to play with. I liked her a lot. Really sorry about what happened to her."

"And the other one?" Amanda had reportedly frequented this place, too.

Will sighed. "I hate to speak ill of the dead, but Mandy was a difficult one. She was the kind of woman who was sweet as pie to a man, but the minute they were gone she was mean. As far as I can tell she pretty much bullied every sub in the place. If it was just her, I would say it was about revenge, but Tanya and the other girl are in the mix. Do you think I should warn the guys, too? The new bouncer and the bartender are a couple. Pretty sure the bartender is the bottom. Well, I can't tell. They're both awfully alpha looking. And they're a little awkward around each other. I think the bouncer is the kind who withholds affection as punishment. The bartender tried to hug him and the bouncer practically jumped out of his skin."

So Sean and Li needed to work on their cover. "Well, maybe we can talk them into a scene so they can work out their issues."

Karina coughed but it sounded suspiciously like "video." On that he and his sweet sub were in perfect accord. That shit was going on YouTube.

"How many uncollared subs do you think come in and out of here on a good night?"

Will shrugged a little. "No more than ten or so. You know how it is. There are always more Doms than female subs. We see some gay couples. Lots of submissive men looking for Dommes. The usual for a place like this. There are also a lot of tourists. Honestly, I've been talking to a couple of the guys I've met here and we're thinking of leaving. This is not the safest place to play. I don't like the way they run things. I only came because I have nowhere else to go. Luckily, I met this little thing." He smiled down on his sub with what seemed like pure affection. "I think it might be time to put my money where my mouth is and open a space where we're all a little safer."

Every instinct he had said the guy was in for heartache because he was being honest. But a good cop didn't just follow instinct. If he was in this club, he was a suspect. He would need to figure out his last name and start a folder on him. Sean and Liam were doing the same thing. By the end of the night, they would have a list of people to research and a list of possibles to let Eve sort through.

"Well, good luck with that. Karina and I are going to just go with the flow." Until he could get her out of here and back to Sanctum where they would be safe. And where they wouldn't have a contract in place because he'd put an end date on their relationship. It had seemed like a good idea at the time, but now the thought made him grumpy. "Come along, gorgeous. We have a scene to perform in a couple of minutes."

Will frowned his way. "Are you sure that's a good idea? I've heard that all the girls who were killed had just performed heavy scenes. I'm keeping Starr away from that for a while."

"Maybe you should keep her at home then." If he was so worried about it, that seemed like the way to go.

For the first time Starr reacted, whimpering a little and grabbing her Dom's thigh.

"Hush, baby. It's fine." When he looked back, he sighed. "She needs this. Besides, I have a lot of friends here and I want to make sure they're all right. I specifically came to find Karina. She's so kind to everyone. I couldn't stand the thought of her being a victim."

"Well, now you know she's got a protector."

"I know she has a Dom," Will said gravely. He nodded toward Karina. "If you need anything, Karina, you know where to find me. Come along, Starr. Let's find a place to watch the scenes."

Karina's head came up as they walked away. "It's not him."

"How do you know?" He really hadn't liked the way the fucker looked at his sub and offered her help. She was wearing a collar. She only needed help from the man who had put it there. Of course, it wasn't like they'd had a ceremony. It had been perfunctory. He'd handed her the collar and she'd put it on.

Why hadn't he put it on her? Why hadn't he stood behind her and pushed her hair out of the way gently before clasping the collar around her pretty throat himself?

"Will's a good guy."

He felt his jaw go hard. "I ask again. How do you know? Have you played with him?"

Her hand came up to grasp his. "No, Derek. I've just talked to him. I've watched him carefully. He's very good with ropes so I had him down as a suspect. I've gotten to know him and I really think his intentions are good. His sub, on the other hand, is a problem."

His jealousy was going to be the death of him. He helped her up, shoving the emotion aside because it had no place between them. He didn't have the right to get jealous and apparently no reason at all. He believed her. "How is she a problem? Beyond the cheating?"

"Well, that's pretty horrible, but she's manipulating him. The only time she shows any emotion is when she wants him to do something.

I don't get why he can't see it."

Derek did. "Because he cares about her. Probably thinks he loves her. He doesn't want to see it. Sometimes it's just easier to pretend that everything is okay. What do you know about his time in the lifestyle?"

"I've been careful about questioning him. I can't ask directly. Everything I know I've figured out from our talks." Her fingers slid through his, making a place for her hand, fitting together easily.

"Just give me your impressions." She'd been a working PI for a very long time. She knew people. "Come on. We really do have to scene and I really am going to tear into your sweet ass with a paddle."

Her brows came over her eyes in a deep *V*. "Why?"

He leaned over and kissed her. He could do that now. He could kiss her whenever he fucking felt like it and he felt like it a lot. "Because you are a brat. And because we'll both like it."

He didn't say the real reason. He would prefer to play with her privately, but they needed to work. They had to put her on display. He fucking hated the idea and yet he got hard at it, too. Karina was going to make him crazy.

"I'm not a brat." But she went on her tiptoes and brushed her lips against his. "But I will give you my impressions about Will. He's fairly new to the lifestyle and like most newbies, he's still infatuated with everything about it. That's likely why he's found someone like Starr."

He started toward the scene space, a raised stage in the middle of the room. There were a couple of scene spaces, but he'd signed them up for the main stage. He needed to make her the center of attention. He stopped. "Why don't we go home, Karina?"

She pulled on his hand and he turned. "I'm going to be okay, Derek."

He nodded. It was stupid. He was behaving entirely unprofessionally. "Of course you are."

She leaned in, hugging him. She always seemed to know when he needed affection. "I will because you're here with me. You're going to be okay, too. Now we have a couple of seconds while they clean up. Please tell me they're cleaning up."

"I have a box of antibacterial wipes in my kit." He fully intended to use them.

"Is it wrong that I find it sexy when you clean things?" Her eyes sparkled. She was a flipping jewel in the middle of the trash heap. "So do you get what I mean about Starr?"

"Yeah, every Dom finds a woman like her in the beginning. We mistake submissive behavior for true submission. We think because a woman says she needs a top that she really does." He'd made the mistake. More than once. It was why he was taking Karina at face value. She played. Her submission didn't go beyond that and he should always remember.

"He hasn't been in the lifestyle long, though I would bet he'd always been interested. He's never been married, but he came out of a long-term relationship and I think that's the same time he decided to give the lifestyle a go."

"Are you profiling or do you know that for a fact?" He stared at the stage. They were almost ready. Desire warred with fear as he thought about what he was about to do. He was going to put her on display, show the entire crowd that she belonged to him, that she submitted to him. He would spank her, flog her if he wanted to. She'd checked public sex as one of her wild turn-ons. Of course, she'd also checked that she was experienced in it.

Who had she had public sex with? Not at Sanctum. She kept that to privacy rooms. It must have been her husband. Her husband had been her Dom. Had he been the one to introduce her to the lifestyle? He was so curious and she wouldn't talk about him. Every time he brought up the subject, she turned the conversation to something else.

"I had a long talk with Will. We went to a late dinner one night and before you get your chest all puffed out, Starr was with us, though apparently she doesn't eat. I think he was feeling me out for a friend of his."

"As long as he wasn't feeling you up." The words were out of his mouth before he could think to keep them in.

"You are a possessive ape-man, Brighton." But she kissed him again.

"All this affection isn't going to save you." She was getting to him. Every damn time she touched him, he went a little deeper. He'd talked about how dumbass new Doms were, but he felt like one now. Stupid. Curious. So desperate he couldn't help himself.

"I don't want to be saved. Didn't you hear? I'm a masochist. I've been coming to this club night after night and I haven't played once." She gave him a wink. "And I've never really played with you, Brighton. That one time doesn't count. If you play the way you fuck, I'm going to die on that stage. Bring your *A* game."

She started toward the stage, her hips swaying, and his cock jumped in his leathers. It didn't care that he was about to make her a target.

It only wanted what he wanted—to be with her. He clutched his kit and followed her onstage.

\* \* \* \*

*The job. Think about the job.*

Karina couldn't think about anything but the fact that she was about to do a public scene with Derek Brighton. And Derek Brighton was jealous. Of her.

There had been no way to miss his caveman-like reaction to Master Will. How could she explain that the man was nice but he moved her not an inch? Yes, he was attractive. Yes, he was muscular and dominant, but he wasn't a grumpy clean freak so he didn't do it for her.

Industrial music thudded through the club and she took a deep breath, prepping herself for a nice few moments. It didn't matter that everyone was watching her. It didn't even matter that the killer could be watching her. She was safe here and she wouldn't let anyone take that away from her.

"Do you want to know what's going to happen?" Derek's voice was low in her ear. They stopped right in front of the stairs.

She shook her head. If she trusted Derek, then she didn't need to know what was going to happen. There wasn't a doubt in her head that he remembered her hard and soft limits. He wouldn't do anything to her that wouldn't ultimately bring her pleasure or joy.

He towered over her even in her heels. His hand found her hair, gently tugging her face up to meet his. "Thank you, gorgeous. I can't tell you what your trust means to me. Stay here while I set up. Sean and Li are both watching, but they're also watching the crowd. If anyone even touches you the wrong way, you scream. And every way is the wrong way."

She felt her lips tug up. Caveman. "No touching. Got it."

He kissed her forehead and then strode up the stairs because Derek never just walked. He stomped and marched and stalked. And cleaned. She couldn't help but smile as he proved he really did carry around a package of antibacterial wipes. He set his kit down and started to work on the bench where he would very likely make her ass red.

She felt someone bump against her and glanced up. Liam didn't look her way. He merely stared out over the crowd and let her know he was there. She looked around and saw Sean was on the opposite side of the crowd doing the same thing. No one would get past those men. It was all right for her to find her peaceful place, all right to take a few minutes of blissful rest.

Every muscle in her body seemed to melt. So much of her day was spent tense and anxious. She always had to be on watch.

Sometimes she wondered what she would have done if she hadn't found this space, hadn't allowed Kevin to take her to a place where she could center and find peace. At first it had seemed freaky and weird, but she'd been so in love with him she would have done anything to keep him. She'd been a kid barely out of rehab, holding on to the only family she'd been able to find. The first time she'd let him tie her up and spank her, she'd shook and cried and somewhere in the middle of it, she'd stopped. Her brain had relaxed, shut down to a place where she could simply feel.

Kevin had worked hard to get her there. Derek merely had to look at her the right way and she melted. How could he do that to her? Why did she trust the man who was likely going to break her heart in the end?

"Karina?" He stood at the top of the steps, a length of rope in his hands.

Everything inside her responded to him. She took his hand and climbed the steps.

He led her to the center of the stage, placing her in front, showing her off. His lips were right against her ear as his hands went to the hooks on the front of the corset. She'd loosened the laces before coming out for the scene, knowing what he would very likely want to do. They needed to make her a big target.

"I'm here with you," he whispered. "Let me take you out of yourself for a while."

She let herself relax again. It didn't matter why they were here. They were here and they had tonight and she wouldn't look beyond that. She knew better than anyone else that tomorrow was a promise that didn't always get kept. She really only had the now and she wanted Derek. She wanted to be his sub and take everything he could give her.

His hands moved, pushing in and then pulling out, expertly

unhooking the corset and setting her skin free. He set the corset aside and then his fingers were playing along the indentions where the corset had been tight against her skin. "I'm going to give you more of these. You're going to be so pretty when I'm through."

She shivered at the thought. He was going to tie her up. He was going to bind her with his rope and she would be utterly dependent on him. She'd watched him bind other subs, his hands so careful as he worked his ropes.

"Silk." He let the rope dangle between her breasts, drawing it up from behind. Every inch he pulled lit up her skin. Her nipples peaked and she felt the whole world going soft and a little out of focus. "I've never used it before. I won't use it on anyone but you. Submit to me, Karina."

There was only one answer. "Yes."

"Hands together, behind your back." His voice had gone deep, deeper than usual. Like rich dark chocolate deep.

He was a master, wrapping the rope perfectly, binding her tight. She let her eyes drift closed, shutting out everything but the feel of his hands on her, the sound of his voice, the rope sliding along her skin. He moved her breasts into place so his ropes would frame them, showing her off. Even without looking, she knew the pattern he was creating. Tortoiseshells. It would form a dress of sorts. Her Master draping her in a garment of his choosing. He worked slowly, methodically. She could almost see his face. He got so serious during a scene. She loved the way his brow furrowed, his jaw tightening as he worked the complex knots.

It bit in some places, holding her limbs to her body, and after a while, she was able to imagine that the rope was the only thing holding her together. Her body was light. If she was unbound, she would float away, drifting through the air.

"Karina, are you with me?"

She nodded.

"Then let me help you to the bench. You know what you're being punished for?"

She let her eyes drift open, glancing at him. He was so big and strong, with his chest covered in a leather vest. "I do, Master."

She was being punished because she liked it. She was being punished because it was part of their cover. She was being punished because if he didn't spank her soon she was going to die.

Glancing down, she saw the way he'd trussed her up. She'd been right about the tortoiseshell pattern. Her arms were behind her back and her whole torso had been bound in the lovely circular pattern. She was held tight, but nothing that would cut off her circulation. He'd avoided her joints, but paid particular attention to her breasts. They were out there for the world to see, boldly thrust up by her Master's ropes.

And he was a kind Dom. He'd given her a perfectly placed crotch knot. Yep. Even as he helped her to the spanking bench, she could feel it moving against her clitoris. She'd wondered why he'd left her thong on, but now she knew. He'd wanted that barrier of silk to aid in the rope's slide.

He placed her on the bench, her breasts on either side of the thin, padded seat. She let her cheek rest against the leather, perfectly satisfied that it was clean and ready for her. Derek wouldn't allow anything less.

How long had it been since a man had taken care of her the way Derek was? Maybe never, she had to admit. Kevin had been loving and kind, but he hadn't had the attention to detail Derek had.

Maybe it was time to stop comparing them and let them be. Her two lovers. Maybe it was time to simply admit that she was lucky to have had them both.

"You're already crying. Use your safe word if you're scared." His hand was in her hair.

She had to make him understand. "It's not bad. It's the only...."

"It's the only time you can let yourself go. Then let me help you. Let me give you what you need. Forget about everything except what you need." His hand touched the cheek of her ass and he began.

He was methodical. He was devious. He never struck the same place in the same way. He gave her long, hard smacks that shook her body and then short, sharp ones to keep her on edge. Every single smack made the knot press against her clit. Pleasure warred with pain, but at the heart of all of it was that amazing sense of relief she found. It was so much stronger with Derek. She'd always needed this, craved it like the addict she was, but this particular drug was stronger than the rest. The other Doms had gotten her to a place she needed to go, but it was like a stop along the way to the destination she hadn't known she was searching for. Derek took her to heaven. Nirvana. Anywhere a woman found herself, that was where he took her.

She didn't even realize when he'd stopped. She was so deep into her subspace that she wondered how much time had passed between the spanking and his calling her name.

It was dangerous. She slipped into subspace so quickly with him that it could be bad if he weren't so damn trustworthy.

She'd been a bitch to him in the past and yet she knew he would never hurt her, never take advantage of her trust. She'd wronged him, made his life hell because he pissed her off, and yet his hands were so gentle on her.

"Karina, I'm done. I can't do any more without hurting you."

And he would never hurt her even when she didn't care. "Let me serve you."

"Karina, you don't have to."

She wanted to give back to him. He was such a giving Dom. She'd been around long enough to know the type. Some Doms lived to be serviced. Not this one. Derek needed to be needed. He needed a sub who thrived under his care, his affection. But what she'd figured out about service tops was that they often forgot about their own needs. They gave and gave to their bottoms without requesting return.

She wanted to give to him, to finish the unspoken agreement between them. They had a contract but it was heavily weighted in her favor. She was the sub. She controlled the bargain.

Love was something different. She was suddenly pretty damn sure she loved Derek Brighton.

"I want to. I want to serve my Master openly. I want everyone to see how much I submit. Derek, please."

This wasn't about the case. It was about him. He'd given her more than she could have imagined. More affection. More honesty. More truth about himself. He'd held up his end of the bargain. He seemed to enjoy lying in bed with her and talking. He'd told her about his life, and she loved hearing his stories. He was a hero. He deserved so much and she wanted to give it to him.

His hands went around her waist and he picked her up without even a grunt of recognition to her weight. He just lifted her and placed her where he wanted her to go.

On her knees. In front of him.

Yes, that did it for her. He'd been so open with her pleasure. Every time he'd taken her, he'd gone down and licked and sucked until she screamed. But he'd been in charge and he'd pleasured her, only taking his own after he'd secured her orgasm. She wanted to give back, wanted him to know it was okay to take from her, too. And damn, but she wanted a taste of that man. She'd only ever sucked one other cock. She'd never wanted another.

"Serve me, gorgeous. Let them all see that you belong to me." His hands went to the ties on his leathers.

And she watched as he released his cock. Usually he was all over her. He never gave her a moment to really stare at him. She took it now. He was beautiful. His cock was freaking gorgeous. Thick and long, he had a beautiful cock. With a plum-shaped head and pretty pink skin, she couldn't help but have her mouth water.

He stepped in, bringing that glorious cock closer to her mouth. He'd helped her to her knees. The dress he'd wound around her body stopped at the middle of her thighs so she had some wiggle room. She let her thighs fall open slightly, allowing the knot on her clit to tighten. So good. She only had to move up and down to work the knot. Her sweet Master had prepared her for pleasure.

His hand was on his cock, that big hand that had brought her such peace. He stroked his cock, running his hand all along from the base to the gorgeous bulbous head of his dick. He stroked himself a few times, allowing her to watch him before pushing his dick to her lips. "Suck me."

There was nothing she wanted more. She wanted to suck him, to make him crazy, to make him come. She wanted to taste him the way he'd tasted her. He'd spent so much time on her that she felt the need to pay him back. Like a lover. Like a Dom.

She leaned forward, deeply loving the way his bindings held her. She couldn't touch him with anything but her mouth. Her hands were securely bound along with the rest of her torso. She could feel his mark on every inch of her skin. It was like he touched her everywhere.

She licked the head of his dick. So long. It had been so long since she'd performed this service and now she remembered why she liked it. She wanted to pay back her Dom. She wanted to be a part of a D/s couple, to be necessary.

A low groan came from his throat and she knew she was doing the right thing. She was doing the thing that brought her Dom pleasure. She sucked the head of his cock inside and let her tongue worry the soft, sweet underside. There was a delicious $V$ on the underside of his dick that she could play with. His fingers found her hair and she knew damn well she was making him crazy. His pelvis thrust forward, a groan coming from his throat.

He pulled on her hair, forcing his dick in farther.

She could taste his pre-come, knew he wouldn't last long under her teeth and tongue. He might talk a good game about wanting a sweet sub who never ever did what she wasn't told to do, but he liked it when she was rough with him. She gave him the bare feel of her teeth along his cock and she felt him pulse in her mouth.

"Take more." He shoved his dick farther in, his hands tangling in her hair.

The desperate quality to his voice made her pussy soften. She worked her pelvis up and down, loving how the knot felt against her clit as she sucked his cock.

She let her tongue coat his cock. He would never fit perfectly. He was way too big for that. She had to relax her damn jaw to get him even halfway in. He stroked her, setting a sweet rhythm. Her tongue whirled. She ran it all around his cock and sucked deep.

Over and over she drew him inside. His tangy essence coated her tongue and she sucked harder, taking him deeper into her mouth. Inch by inch she worked him to the back of her throat. She sucked him hard, loving the flavor of his pre-come. She wanted to touch him, but his bindings forced her to focus on him, on the feel of his dick on her tongue, the way he held her head, the taste of him. She pushed all thoughts of herself down. He'd done that with her. He'd focused on her so it was easy, so easy to give him her attention.

*Down and back. Down and back.* She loved how his hands tangled harder in her hair. Like he couldn't stop himself. Every motion brought her closer to climax because that knot he'd tied rubbed her clit.

Pleasure swamped her, making her work him even harder. The music thrummed through her system, pulsing against her skin. The fact that there was an audience only made it better. They might not see his climax, but she would give them a show. She was powerful and beautiful in the moment. It didn't matter what anyone else thought. It only mattered what she felt. And she felt like she was ten feet tall. Derek groaned and shoved his cock in, harder and faster than before. He was losing that control of his. He always took such care with her. It meant something that he would let go.

It meant that he was hers.

It might not last forever, but in this moment, he belonged to her. Her sweet Master.

She inhaled his cock, working the knot at her clit the whole time. As she drew him to the back of her throat, she felt the orgasm bloom. He'd worked his magic and he didn't have to keep a hand on her.

He'd set her up to come to her pleasure. Every knot he'd built had brought her to a sweet spot. She pulled hard on his cock, thrilled when she tasted the first of his come on her tongue.

"Karina!" He shouted her name as he shoved his cock deep. Over and over he pulsed in her mouth, giving her everything he had.

He held her hair, but it was gentler now, his cock a presence but he'd relaxed as he'd given up his come. She licked and sucked and enjoyed her power. Her orgasm flushed through her system, making the world a lovely place.

"Thank you, gorgeous," he said softly.

She let his cock slip away, knowing she would have him again. When she opened her eyes, she glanced around. Every person in the club seemed to be watching them. Derek smoothed her hair back. He helped her stand and started to unwind the ropes he'd bound her up in.

"You were perfect." He whispered the words in her ear.

She was the perfect sub? Or the perfect bait?

She didn't ask, but wondered all the while who had been watching them.

# Chapter Eight

Derek shook his head as he refused a second cup of coffee. Maia frowned at him, her eyes widening.

"Are you sure? You've only had one. You usually drink four or five cups before noon. Are you on some weird cleanse?" She kept the coffee for herself, but stared at him, suspicion plain in her eyes.

"I don't need it. I only drink that crap for the caffeine." He actually didn't love the taste, but he needed to wake up usually. He turned back to the door, hoping Karina would waltz back in and save him. No such luck. He'd been left alone in the McKay-Taggart conference room with his ex-wife, the two Texas Rangers, and their insanely obnoxious forensics guy who apparently had exciting news about old e-mails.

He didn't need coffee. He needed a beer.

Maia sank into her seat, her perfect nails drumming along the tabletop. "I know. You don't sleep well. Did you finally give in and get a prescription?"

He felt a slow smile slide across his face. He didn't need a pill. He had Karina. A week in Karina's crappy bed had his back aching, but it had oddly given him a more peaceful sleep than he'd had in years. He'd had the dream once more since that first night, but Karina had flipped him over and gotten him in a nice nelson hold. When he'd woken up, she'd been cool and collected and had calmly told him to go back to sleep.

Yeah, he'd turned the tables on her and had her screaming out his name in about five minutes. And then he had happily gone back to sleep. Fucking Karina was way better than a sleeping pill.

"I don't want to know what that's about," Clayton Hill said, sitting back in his chair. "Is there anything to report, Lieutenant?"

Now it was Derek's turn to frown. While he'd settled into a weirdly comfortable domesticity with Karina, they had gotten nowhere on the case front. "We went to the club four of the five nights it was open. She wasn't even accosted by anyone but a drunk kid outside the building. I even left her alone for an hour on the last night."

"Did you?" Harris asked. "Because I'm betting you simply took a step back and then loomed over her like a predatory hawk. I saw the tapes from the feed. Your version of letting her be on her own is to walk a step behind her."

"Well, I wasn't going to totally walk away," he grumbled under his breath because there was some truth to Harris's words. He and Karina had a long argument when she realized he'd never really walked away. What had she expected him to do? Take a break while there was a killer stalking her?

Hill shook his head. "I can't blame you for that."

"I can," Maia said, her temper obviously on a short leash, but there was nothing new in that. "You're letting this asshole get away because you want to get laid, Derek. She's not fragile. She's a tough bitch. She can handle this guy. Look, I let you put O'Donnell and Taggart the Lesser Ass on this. Use them or I'll pull you from this case."

"I don't think that's really in your purview," Hill said laconically. He yawned as though the whole argument bored him.

Watts rolled his eyes. "Yeah, I think your part comes later, Ms. Brighton."

God, he wished she'd changed her damn name.

"My part comes never if Derek doesn't do his job," she shot back.

"I'm with the Ice Queen," Harris said. "The lieutenant is thinking with his dick. That would be fine if his dick had a high IQ. We're going to lose this guy if we don't dangle the bait a little harder."

"I don't know about that," Eve said as she walked in the room, following her husband. She was the reason they were meeting at McKay-Taggart rather than in his office or the Grand Prairie Ranger office. Eve sat down when Alex held her chair out and immediately got to the point. "I don't think having a male around is going to scare this killer off. He's not swayed by opportunity. He's goal oriented. He won't give up because she's suddenly got a boyfriend. I actually think it will make him work harder."

Hill sat up, giving Eve his full attention. "You don't think we should make Ms. Mills a bigger target?"

"I think he's picked his target and he won't be swayed," Eve said.

Alex sat down beside his wife. He was dressed in a suit, an odd sight since Alex McKay tended to be a bit more casual. He and his wife were both dressed for some sort of business meeting. "The worry is that he'll be patient. The longer he waits, the more you and Karina will tend to let your guard down. I want you to really think about this. How does this work if he waits a month? Two months? Six months?"

The idea put a knot in his stomach for more than one reason. The chief one being it didn't sound so bad. He wouldn't be able to leave her so he would have to move in. He couldn't keep living out of his gym bag. He would pick up his things and hang them next to hers in the closet because it was the practical thing to do.

Of course, if it lasted too long, they should just move. Her place was cramped. He needed an office. They should look at two bedrooms closer to the station. He hated to have to drive to work. No more than two stops away would be ideal.

He stopped because he wasn't moving in with Karina. *Fuck.* He was getting comfortable with a woman he knew damn well wasn't good for him. He was making all the same mistakes again. He'd put up with Maia because it was easier than doing the hard thing and taking the hit.

Although Karina was turning out to be so different than he'd expected.

"Derek?" Maia huffed a little. "Are you going to join us?"

"I was thinking." About anything but the fact that someone was stalking Karina. "Little Tag and O'Donnell can't watch her the way I can."

"Oh, for god's sake, Derek. You're acting like she's a civilian. She's not. She can handle herself. Slap a bug in her tits and get her out there. I want this guy brought in. I am not going to wait six months for my case." She stood up, her face a bright red. "And I will use my influence to have you pulled off the case if I have to because don't think I don't know what's going on. You're behaving in a wholly unprofessional fashion."

"Yes, because fucking on the job is so out of fashion in your world." He was glad Karina wasn't in here now because she likely would have been embarrassed. He just expected Maia to lash out when things weren't going well.

She stared at him. "I can handle it, Brighton. I can handle it because I would never let it affect my work. She's fucking with your head. What are you doing? Do you even know?"

"I'm doing my job, which is to make sure she doesn't get killed."

"That's where you're wrong. It's your job to catch this fucker, but you seem to have forgotten that. You should remember or you'll find yourself off the case." She stormed out in true Maia fashion.

Harris sighed and sat back. "It's like watching a soap opera. It's kind of beautiful. She's the villain by the way."

Yeah, he didn't need anyone to tell him that. "You're not exactly the hero yourself, Harris."

The little shit grinned in a way that let Derek know he'd just fallen into a trap. "Oh, I don't know that I'd say that. Did you realize Karina has a couple of e-mail addresses she doesn't check very often? There's the address for her business and she has a personal address, but seriously there's almost nothing on that one. She's all business, although surprisingly huggy for a tough private investigator. I was expecting her to go all Mickey Spillane on everyone, but it's mostly hand holding and shit."

He should have known someone would dig into her e-mail. "Is there a point to this?"

"She has an account from a few years before." He frowned a little. "Interesting stuff. Let's say she had some seriously unsavory contacts back in New York. And her record. Yeah, gotta love a chick with her issues. I'm going with the Ice Queen on this one. That girl can handle herself."

Record? Karina had a police record? "What are you talking about?"

"Harris, you say another word and I'll fire you myself. Those records were sealed for a reason and they have nothing to do with this case," Watts said, his eyes narrowing.

"Firing him would be too much paperwork." Hill's words came out with lazy menace.

"I hate it when they do that. It really freaks me out. Fine." Harris frowned. "I won't spill on her deeply interesting youth, but I am going to talk about her e-mail. Our boy isn't as patient as we thought. He's sent her two love notes."

A chill went across Derek's skin. He wanted to protest and say that any goddamn record of Karina's was relevant as hell to him. Sealed records. There were only a couple of reasons for them. She was underage when she'd committed the offense or she'd made a hell of a deal.

"Let me see the note he sent." It didn't matter. Her secrets were hers and he didn't give a shit. Except he'd told her his secrets. He'd lain in bed with her and talked about Afghanistan and all the shit that happened to him there. She wouldn't even talk about her marriage. He still had no idea what had gone wrong because he'd made the decision to live in the now. The past didn't matter. They had no real future. He'd wanted to indulge in the intimacy of the moment, but even that was coming back to bite him in the ass.

Harris passed over his tablet.

*Hello, bitch. Did you think I wasn't watching? I see all the whores. All your perverted ways are open to me as you will be open to me when I take you into the final judgment. You will be bound and found guilty of your sins. I'm watching. He can't save you from me. Tell your friends, I'm coming for them, too.*

He took a deep breath to banish the sick feeling in the pit of his stomach.

"Derek?" Eve held out her hand.

He passed the tablet and sat back. Somehow the danger surrounding the case had seemed a distant thing until that moment. It had been quiet, peaceful even. "How would he have found that e-mail account? And why now? He didn't send notes to the others."

Eve sent the tablet down the row, giving everyone the joy of reading the fucker's message. "He's reacting to stimuli. He's obviously noticed something is different and he's upping his game. Or perhaps he truly wants her and us to understand why she's going to be killed."

"You just said he was patient. This doesn't seem patient to me." Sometimes Derek hated the whole profiling thing. He understood the need, but it was a little like reading tea leaves in his opinion.

"He can be both," Eve replied. "And this is a good thing. The more data he gives us, the better chance we have to figure out who this is."

And the quicker he would have to make a serious decision. If there was any decision at all to be made. They had agreed to take it easy. Once the case was over there really wouldn't be any reason for him to stay at her place except the sex. If she could go back to Sanctum, would she want him anymore? Or would she go back to playing around with the Doms there?

Would he be able to watch her? Would she be under Simon Weston's flogger the minute he got back from England?

And what the fuck had she been arrested for?

He hated not knowing. He hated the fact that the Rangers knew more about her than he did.

Fifteen minutes later, they were breaking up but there was still no sign of Karina. She'd walked off to look for O'Donnell and now his brain was playing a nasty game with him. They were comfortable together. She was far more comfortable with O'Donnell than she was with him.

Alex McKay shook the hand of Tyler Watts as he was the last one to leave. Eve had led them out and through the glass windows of the conference room, he could see her talking to them.

"How are you holding up?" Alex leaned over the conference table, gathering his notes.

"I'm fine."

"I heard you moved in with Karina." Alex was only a year or two older than him, but Derek suddenly got the feeling this was going to be more of a big brother talk.

"I didn't move in. It's a long-term stakeout and protection gig." The last thing he needed was a bunch of gossip. When this was over, he didn't want the members of Sanctum doing a postmortem on his non-relationship with Karina.

He didn't want them talking about how it was more of a relationship than he'd had in years. It was work and a little casual fun.

"So you're sleeping on the couch then."

Yeah, Alex was definitely in big brother mode. "That's really none of your business. That's between me and my sub."

Alex's eyebrow rose. Shit. He was a mess. He wasn't thinking about what he was saying. "Your sub? I thought this was a job."

Derek stalked to the window, wishing like hell Alex had just walked out and left him alone. "We agreed to play together for the duration of the assignment. I thought it was best she not be left alone at night. We both realized it would be hard to keep our hands off each other, so we made a mature decision to enjoy the time we have."

"Yes, mature. Nothing about this is mature, Derek. Look, Ian should be the one having this talk with you, but he's living out his fantasy in a giant floating dungeon in the middle of the Baltic, so it has to be me."

"I've already gotten the lecture from O'Donnell and Little Tag. I don't need another one."

"Yeah, Li and Sean are going to come down on Karina's side

because they don't know you the way Ian and I do. I'm worried about both of you, but mostly you."

Derek frowned and turned around. "Why the hell would you worry about me?"

"Karina's going to be okay in the end because if you break her heart, she's going to go to her friends and she'll cry it out and lean on them. You will go back into your shell and pretend nothing is wrong. You'll go right back to the club and keep searching for your dream cipher and we're all praying you don't find her, though there is a bet that one day you'll show up with a blow-up doll from Japan and the two of you will be very happy."

"Fuck you, McKay."

Alex held up his hands. "I'm being honest with you."

He was sick of this argument. "I don't understand how knowing what I want makes me the bad guy here. I know what didn't work. I know I don't want to go through that again. I don't want to put anyone through that again."

"Karina isn't Maia," Alex said softly. "Not even close."

"Yeah, well, Maia wasn't fucking Maia when I married her. What do you know about Karina's arrest record?"

He shook his head. "I know that Ian likely has the whole story but if he hasn't told me then I don't need to know."

"How can you say that?"

"Because I trust him. At the end of the day, I trust her, too. She's proven herself to me. Look, I don't have to know every single thing about a person to know who she is. I know all the facts about Eve. I know every single thing that's happened to her. I know her stories, and there is a core to that woman that I won't ever truly understand. She's a beautiful mystery. We've been in bad places, but somehow we figured a way to grow together. Everyone changes. The key is to love her enough to change with her. If you get this dream sub who mindlessly obeys you, you'll never change at all. You'll never change for her, never truly sacrifice, and then you will never really love her."

Did Alex think that hadn't gone through his head? He'd been over and over it and he'd decided Karina was another one of life's traps. He would love her, worship her, and she would be okay with that until she found something better. Or worse. She would expect him to join her corral of former lovers. "I tried the love thing before. It didn't work."

Alex chuckled but it was a frustrated sound. "Because it wasn't love. Not really. You were a kid when you married Maia, and then you were pretty much broken and you still haven't put yourself back together. If you think this perfect sub of yours is going to be the one to do it, you're smoking something a cop shouldn't smoke. Karina is smart and strong and if you play your cards right, she'll be a partner to you. Not like Maia was. You're judging marriages by your own. Maia is an out of control top who likes to play at being submissive. Karina is a sub in desperate need of a Master who loves and appreciates her strengths and protects her from her weaknesses."

"From what I can tell, Karina has no weaknesses." It bugged him. Beyond the dust bunnies she allowed free range of her place, she was perfect. She could handle him physically. Her clients seemed to think she walked on water. Everyone loved Karina. She didn't really need him.

"Oh, watch her. Stop looking at the surface and get to the real woman underneath. Take off your poop-colored glasses and see things as they really are. If you do, you might figure out that the perfect sub has been standing in front of you all along. And that's all I'm going to say."

He sighed with relief. At least the detectives under his command never tried to give him love advice. "Thank god."

Alex laughed, this time a purely happy sound. "You'll be on my side of the table one day if you're lucky and some sad sack just like you is going to need advice. And you'll give it to him. Take care of her."

Alex started for the door, and Derek tried really hard to let him go. Really hard. "Alex?"

"Yep?"

"How do I handle the jealousy?" It burned through his gut. It was wrong because god knew he'd been with plenty of women, but what Maia had done to him had left a hole a mile wide that he wasn't sure how to fill in. Maybe everyone was right and he was interested in a twenty-four seven relationship because he thought it would make him safe.

He wanted Karina. It was time to be honest with himself. He didn't want to walk away, but he wasn't sure he could stay.

"Why would you be jealous?"

Was the man going to make him say it? "Look, I know it's normal to have casual sex when you don't have a permanent partner. I've done it myself so it makes me the bad guy to say this, but it bugs me that Karina hangs out with the guys so much."

Alex shrugged. "She works with us, man. Are you jealous because she used to play with Liam?"

"And Sean a couple of years back, and now it's Simon. I know she's played with Ian." He kind of hated every single man who had ever touched her. This was why he shouldn't get too close to her. She made him feel things he never wanted to feel again.

"Yes. Ian still scenes with her when she needs a partner. Charlotte understands Karina's needs and encourages Ian to work with her. Look, I don't know why, but Karina needs to scene a couple of times a week. There's nothing more to it. If you would top her, I think you would find as long as you were around she wouldn't want anyone but you."

"And when I'm not? I'm just supposed to be okay with that? I'm supposed to let Simon or Big Tag fuck around with my sub because she needs it?"

Alex's eyes went wide. "What? Maybe we need to get on the same page here. We're talking about scenes. Not fucking. We're talking about flogging and spanking and the occasional whipping if she wants it. Do you honestly think Ian's screwing Karina? Have you met his wife? First, she would seriously take off his balls and second, she would likely throw down with Karina." A little smile came over Alex's face. "Of course, if we could get them to do that in a vat of Jell-O, it might be worth it."

Was he the only one who saw it? "She goes to privacy rooms with O'Donnell. She disappears with Simon sometimes."

"I believe you'll find that all they do is talk. Li likes her. So does his wife. And Simon gets a lot out of aftercare, but I would bet my life that he doesn't have sex with her. Trust me, that man has more problems with Chelsea than he can handle." Alex put a hand on his shoulder. "Like I said, take off the glasses you've been viewing the world through for the last several years and see her. See who she really is and then if you still want that sub who will never argue with you, never challenge you, I'll make it my mission to find her. And let the crap Harris talked about go. See Karina for who she is now, not who she used to be."

Alex patted his shoulder in an almost paternal move and then Derek was alone, the door closing behind McKay. Derek stared out the window, the Dallas cityscape in his vision, but all he could see was Karina. He could see her lying beside him, the early morning light caressing her skin. He could stare at her for hours because she was exactly what Alex had called Eve. She was a mystery.

He took a deep breath and let himself be still for a moment. Years had passed, but he suddenly wondered if he'd ever really come home. He'd held himself apart. He'd let himself go numb because it was better than feeling the pain, better than really healing because if he healed he would have to make the decision to go on living.

The week with Karina had shown him he might want more, but he had to know. He had to know what she was hiding before he could make any decisions.

And if she wouldn't tell him the truth, then he was a man who knew how to walk away. Even when it hurt.

* * * *

Karina's cell phone trilled and she glanced down. Damn. Her brother-in-law. She stared at it for a moment. Somehow she didn't want to answer. Her life seemed damn near perfect and he was threatening that. She didn't want to think about the past. Just the now. And the now included another cup of coffee.

She touched the button to send the call to voicemail.

"Yes, the doctor said she's fine. Tristan is doing great. He's so damn cute, Jake. You have to see him." Adam Miles walked into the break room with a tablet in his hand. He was talking into it and it looked like he was using Facetime. "He's gaining weight. He's up to twelve pounds. He kicks those little legs all the time and I can't keep him in bundling to save the kid's life. Our boy's an escape artist."

His baby. Tristan. The little guy was eight weeks old and so cute Karina could hardly stand it. He did kick his little legs and push on his blankets until they were gone. He also sucked on an imaginary nipple in his sleep. So freaking cute.

She nodded Adam's way. Jake was in Europe. They shared a wife. Serena. She wrote romances. Karina liked her books. She gave Adam a smile and he winked her way as he talked into his tablet. "Don't worry about us. The baby's fine. Serena's already working up a storm. We're cool. Just do your job."

"I will. I just wish I was with you guys." Jake's voice came over loud and clear. "How did the checkup go?"

Adam looked up and winked her way. "Can you hold this for me? There's something I need to show Jake."

She was game. She took the tablet and sure enough there was Jake's face staring back at her. "Hey, Jake. How's Europe?"

"Shitty. When I think of a cruise, I think of sunshine and warmth. It's fucking cold in the Baltic. And Big Tag is pretending this is his honeymoon or something. I can't walk into a room without catching sight of him on top of Charlotte. I've seen more of his junk in the last couple of days than in all our years at Sanctum. And Simon and Chelsea are still circling each other warily. Jesse took his training on making towel animals to a new level. He just leaves towel penises in everyone's rooms. You know, the usual stuff."

What Jake didn't mention was that the usual stuff also included near misses with weapons of variable caliber. "You watch your back, Dean."

Jacob Dean smiled. "You watch yours, too. Or rather let the lieutenant watch it. We got the update. You be careful. Any bullets fly your way, you hide behind Brighton. He's tough. He can handle it."

"Okay, turn him my way." Adam had walked back over from his errand at the fridge. He held a small plate in his hand and a fork.

Karina turned the tablet and Adam suddenly had a shit-eating grin on his face as he held up what looked like a slice of lemon cream pie.

"The doctor's visit went great," Adam said. "Perfect. Serena is clear for activities of all kind, so that's why she made me this pie." He took a bite, obviously relishing it. "It's the best pie, Jake. It's after-baby pie. It's 'haven't had any pie in three months' pie. It's all my pie because they don't have this pie in Europe, motherfucker. Mmmmm. Don't worry, I'll eat your share, too."

"You suck!" the voice from the tablet yelled.

Yeah, she was pretty sure Adam wasn't talking about pie. At least not the one in his hands. "You two work out your shit. I have a job to do."

She set the tablet down, grabbed her coffee mug, and started out of the kitchen. The whole time Adam kept telling Jake how good the pie tasted and how long it would be before he got any.

She nearly ran into Liam. Only his big hands stopped her from falling back.

"You all right?" Li asked, steadying her.

She nodded and was grateful she'd only half filled the mug. Derek had brought her coffee in bed this morning. They'd lain there, him watching the morning news and her sipping coffee while she rested against him. It had been peaceful. Just being around her Dom was comfortable. She could let her mind get quiet around him. Not her Dom. He was only hers for a while and she should remember that. "I'm good. What's the word on the searches you ran? I would ask Adam, but he's eating pie."

Li's eyes flared. "Seriously? He's doing that in the break room? Damn, the minute Big Tag leaves, everything goes to hell."

She chuckled. His mind would go there. "Real pie, silly. Serena's not here. He's got Jake on line and he's giving him hell about something."

Liam snorted a little. "Adam can wait a long time for revenge. I'll remember that. Come on to my office. There's been a development."

She followed him down the hall toward his office. "What kind of development?"

"Apparently you got an e-mail. I just talked to Eve. We missed the meeting, but she forwarded the message to me."

She looked back at the conference room, flustered. "How the hell did I miss the meeting? I just went to the bathroom and to get a cup of coffee."

"And I was running a couple of minutes late. I think it was supposed to take longer, but Alex and Eve have some mystery appointment and the ADA got her panties in a wad about something. She was screaming into her cell phone as I walked in and she walked out. Something about a warrant out for her arrest."

Karina gave him her most innocent smile. "Wow. I would not have expected that."

Liam's eyes narrowed. It was times like this she remembered he was a Dom. "What is she wanted for, darlin', because I'm betting this is Karina karma coming to bite her in the ass. She was mean to you?"

"As far as I can tell she's mean to everyone. And she cheated on Derek like five hundred times. Did you know she slept with his brother? While he was overseas. Sometimes the universe gets it wrong and it's up to me to help justice along a little. I think you will discover that she's had her identity stolen by a notorious madam who runs a house of ill repute."

Li shook his head. "You're incorrigible. Derek should tie you to a bench and smack that ass red."

She would probably like that. "It will all get sorted out. I haven't done anything that would really damage her, but if she keeps trying to set Derek up with other subs, I might."

"That's a whole other issue, K. Let's deal with the serial killer first. Do you not check your e-mail accounts?" He opened the door to his office and strode to his desk, letting his muscular body slide into his chair. He flipped open his laptop, his fingers moving over the keyboard of his computer.

"I check my work e-mail." She sunk into the chair in front of his desk and looked at the newest addition to his office. There was a small framed picture on his desk. Karina smiled as she looked at it. A glowing Avery held a tiny bundle in her arms. "How is Aidan?"

Liam's whole face changed when he caught sight of that picture. "He's good. Looks more like his mum every day. He's lifting his little head up and, oh, when that boy cries, he can shake the roof, if you know what I mean."

"I do." Having babies was one of those things she'd given up on. She told herself it was for the best, but watching all her friends with their kids brought back memories of the plans she'd made with Kevin. At least two kids. She didn't care if they were boys or girls, but Kevin said he needed a boy to keep the balance of power in the house.

She wondered how Brighton felt about kids. *Don't even go there.* Shaking off the thought, she got down to business. She couldn't avoid it any longer. "Now, what is this about e-mails?"

He turned his laptop around. "Here it is."

She quickly read through the e-mail. Blah blah bitch. Blah blah whore. Blah blah sins. Typical asshole serial killer stuff. He needed new material. What she found deeply interesting was the address it had posted to. "I haven't used that e-mail in years. I didn't even realize it still existed. If you'll let me hop on, I can try to trace where the message came from."

"I'll get Adam on it as soon as he finishes fucking with Jake. If anyone can track this guy down, it's Adam." He took back his laptop and started typing. "I have other news. I just sent the files to the lieutenant. We've got background checks on almost everyone in the club. It's the usual stuff. We've got a couple of ex-cons, but only one violent offender."

"Who?"

"A man named Jim Benson. The other two were drug arrests, but Jim has an aggravated assault charge on his sheet."

She tried to put a name with a face. "He doesn't ring a bell."

"He's only been in once since we started working, but according to the gossip, he's a regular. He's got an upcoming trial for beating up his ex-girlfriend. They really don't give a shit who they let into this club, do they? I've also got some interesting news on your boy."

"I have a boy?"

"Brighton seems to think you do. He's got a hard-on for this William Daley fellow."

She rolled her eyes. "I've talked to the man a couple of times. Derek is high."

"Derek is jealous. Very jealous from the looks of it." Li sat back. "Are you sure you want to do this with him? You know what he's looking for, right?"

She sighed. She should have expected to get the big brother talk from Li. "I know what he wants. He knows I'm not interested in a true twenty-four seven relationship. I know I'm not his dream sub."

"But he's your dream Dom?"

She liked Liam better when all he did was work and drink beer and go to Hooters. He was more fun then. "Of course not."

"Are you sure?"

"I don't have a dream Dom. I had one. He died. That story is over. Brighton and I are just passing time."

"He didn't sound like he was just passing time when he asked me to look into the good doctor here."

That perked her up. It was way more interesting than talking about her non-relationship with the man who kind of really was her dream Dom. "Will isn't a doctor. He's an EMT."

"Haven't run a trace on him, have you?" Liam sat back with a self-satisfied smile.

Damn, she should have done her own leg work. She hated someone knowing more about her own case than she did. "I haven't had time. I was getting everything ready when the DPD swooped in, and then you took over and I thought it was best to leave the paperwork to you."

"Or you were having too much fun playing house with Brighton."

There was truth to his words. Truth she didn't want to deal with. "Just tell me."

He frowned in that way that let her know she was no fun to play with. "Fine. William Daley. He's thirty-five. Graduated from Johns Hopkins. He's a surgeon."

"Why would he lie and say he's an EMT?"

"My best guess? He's trying to hide his association with the lifestyle from his colleagues. Hospitals are notoriously political. He actually works in Fort Worth, but he drives all the way to Dallas to play. He's trying to keep his lifestyle very private. He's also in the middle of a wrongful death lawsuit. It looks like a woman under his care died. I bet he doesn't want her lawyers to find out and get himself outed as the pervert surgeon who kills young women."

If she had to bet, she would put her money on the fact Will was one of the good ones. "That's not fair."

Liam shrugged. "Not saying it's fair, darlin'. Just saying it's what would happen. His sub, on the other hand, is not quite so well educated. Her real name is Leslie Starling. She's originally from New York. Looks like she made it through a year of community college and then quit. She's had a couple of jobs, but mostly waitressing and serving drinks at golf courses. She worked a couple of jobs on private boats. Do you think that makes her a hooker?"

Liam always went to the worst possible place. "No, I think some crazy rich people can afford to hire staff. My brother-in-law used to captain boats for people. Some of the yachts he worked on had staffs of up to ten people to wait on the owner."

"I bet she still probably slept with them. She's definitely sleeping with the doc. She moved into his condo a month ago. No idea why she suddenly up and moved. She was working in New York and from what I can tell, she just quit and moved here. She got a job at a doctor's office as a receptionist and now she's seeing Master Will. That's probably where they met."

"I know some people in the lifestyle in the city. If she was bottoming there, someone should know her. Maybe I'll give them a call." It was likely nothing, but she liked to follow up when her instincts started to flare. Something was wrong with Starr. She didn't fit, but Karina couldn't put her finger on why.

"Already did," Liam shot back. "I have contacts there, too, and god knows everyone knows Tag." He leaned forward. "No one's heard of her. If she was playing, it wasn't at any of the good clubs. They did ask about you, though. You still have people who care about you up there. Why don't you call them?"

There was something about the way he said it that just let her know. Maybe it was the sympathy that crept into his tone. Maybe it was the way his eyes looked through her. "You know."

He didn't prevaricate. "Are you talking about the fact that you were arrested twice before you were eighteen on drug charges and the only reason you didn't have an adult arrest was the fact that Officer Kevin Mills took you in and got you through rehab?"

She felt her body go numb. Well, if he knew everything it was stupid to lie. "Are you going to tell Tag?"

"Darlin', Tag knows. I knew. This is not information I dug up today. I vetted you before we hired you the first time. I've known for years. What I didn't know was that you don't talk to your friends anymore. They miss you."

She shook her head. "You can't have known. The records were sealed. They were sealed by the courts and then I buried them myself."

"Unsealing records is my job. And you should know nothing ever stays buried. Talking to people is my job. Figuring out who the bad guy is and who the girl who got herself into trouble and was strong enough to get herself out—that's me job, too."

She clenched her fist to stop the fine tremble. If everyone knew, would they look at her differently? "Liam, it was bad."

"Most drug addictions are. And the rate of people who fall off the wagon is high. You didn't. As far as I can tell, you never went back after that last rehab."

She took a deep breath and let it out, trying to calm herself. She could sit around in a meeting and talk for hours, but talking about it to Li was different. "Five thousand four hundred and seventy-nine days sober. And I can't forget to count the days. I do it every morning when I wake up. I shower and brush my teeth and I add another day to the calendar. I look in the mirror and make the decision to not use. Do you understand, Liam? I'm always one step away from falling off the edge."

"Karina, we all are. You seem to think there's something shameful about this. I admire you for getting up and choosing. Why on earth would you hide this?"

"Because I am ashamed. Liam, this is nothing to be proud of."

He shook his head. "You're wrong. You were a kid. You made some rough mistakes but then given what happened to you, I think I understand. You got yourself out. You have nothing, I mean nothing, to be ashamed of. I'm quite proud to call you my friend."

If he kept this up, she was going to lose it. She took the only out she could see. "So I'm not getting canned?"

"Never," Li promised. "But I'm telling you all this because Brighton knows about the sealed records. The fucker forensics guy told him. Eve told me and I thought you should know. He didn't tell Brighton what you've been arrested for, but I doubt it will take him too long to figure it out. Tell him."

"I can't." Because if she did tell him, it would be the end. He might not run, but he would look at her differently. He was looking for a soft, sweet woman, not someone who had spent her youth in and out of foster homes. Not one who had escaped the pain by shoving a needle in her arm.

"Damn it. You're in love with him." Liam sighed. "I don't know that's such a good idea. Don't get me wrong. I like Derek. He's okay, but he's very straight and narrow. He didn't grow up the way the rest of us did. His mum and dad are still married. They still go to church and drag him there on holidays. His brother might have slept with Maia, but they still go to family functions together. Derek still goes to Sunday dinners with the fucker. They're very all-American. I don't want him to break your heart, but you have to be honest with him. It'll be better than him finding out some other way. I don't think you have a thing to be ashamed of, but he might. Best to get it over with and know where you stand."

But she was pretty sure where she would stand. "You're making more out of this than you should, Li. I'm not in love with him. We're just playing around. It's nothing serious so let it go, please."

Liam stood up and crossed the space between them, pulling her up and into a hug. "I'm glad to hear it."

She hugged him back. He knew about her past and he didn't hate her for it. Apparently everyone knew. She'd been hiding in her little closet but the door had been open and everyone was staring inside, likely wondering why she wouldn't come out.

But the idea of Derek finding out? They were happy. Relatively so. Why couldn't she just have her couple of weeks with him? She held on to Liam for a minute, taking comfort knowing he was still her friend.

"Are you done here, Karina?"

She nearly jumped out of Liam's arms. Derek was staring at her with arctic eyes, every muscle in his body tense. She wasn't exactly sure what to say. Defending herself seemed silly. Liam was her friend. She wasn't doing anything wrong. She didn't owe him explanations. "Yes."

"Good, we need to get going. O'Donnell, do you have the files I requested?" Cold as ice. There was no mistaking it. He was pissed.

Liam nodded. "I sent them to you ten minutes ago. Eve is looking through them this afternoon. Hopefully we'll have a couple of prospects Sean and I can look into."

"See that you do. I want to get this done." He turned and Karina was left watching his back as he walked away.

"If you need anything, you know where to come," Liam said. "My and Avery's door is always open."

And that was a good thing, because it felt a little like Derek had slammed his closed.

# Chapter Nine

Derek slammed the car door shut and looked up at Karina's building. It was a piece of crap and he'd already had a talk with the super about getting the lights in the parking lot changed.

He was going to have to leave her soon and he wouldn't have any right to even check in. She would be here all alone with no one to watch out for her. No one to hold her or make sure she was okay. He wouldn't be able to do it because she wouldn't let him. And he couldn't stay involved in another relationship where he didn't matter.

"Are you seriously going to spend the rest of the night not talking to me?"

He was too pissed to talk and his anger wasn't all with Karina. He was pissed as shit at himself because he knew better. He knew better than to let himself really think he could have her for anything beyond a brief moment in time. What the hell had he been thinking? The minute he walked away from her she was in someone else's arms. O'Donnell's. God, he hated the fucker.

And he was pretty sure O'Donnell knew her secrets. "Let's just get upstairs. We don't have long before we need to be at the club."

"Why don't we take the night off?"

He turned to her. "We have a job to do."

"We can take a single night off."

So they could what? So he could fuck her and fall more for her and then watch while she played around with O'Donnell? "The club won't be open Sunday through Tuesday. We can take plenty of time off then." She was leaning against the car door, staring at him with big eyes. So fucking pretty it hurt to look at her. "Unless you have something you want to talk about tonight? Is that it? Do you have something to tell me?"

Maybe if she was just honest with him, they could deal with it. She was so open when he was making love to her, but the minute he wanted to talk she clammed up. She turned it right back around and he found himself talking.

She was hiding something from him and it was starting to make him crazy.

He'd talked to her. Really opened up. He'd told her things he hadn't told another person in the world, but she wouldn't give him anything.

Was she using him? Was he just another in a string of men she played with? Would she expect him to be all buddy buddy with her after they were done? He wasn't sure he could be friends with her.

"No, I just thought we could have dinner and maybe watch some TV. I don't know, Derek. I'm just tired."

And avoiding the subject. "You might be tired, but that won't mean a damn thing to the guy who's after you. I'm wondering how he knew about that e-mail when you seem to have forgotten it."

She shook her head and he couldn't help but think about how the setting sun hit her hair, bringing out the warmth of the color. It always seemed so dark, but when the light hit it just the right way, he could see some auburn in there. "I have no idea. Derek, I'm not trying to hide an e-mail from you. I really haven't checked that account since Kevin died."

"He died?" He'd asked her a couple of times about her marriage, but she'd put him off. Fuck, he'd been sleeping with her and she hadn't even mentioned she was a widow. Her husband had died and she'd never even mentioned it to him.

"Yes. And he died years ago so you can see how long it's been since I checked that e-mail." She was so reasonable. So rational. Like it didn't matter. Did he matter to her at all? "Hey, I'll give you the passwords to all my accounts and then you won't have to hack into them the way that Harris jerk did. I'll let you look through my computer if it makes you feel better." She put a hand on his shoulder. "Come upstairs, Derek. I was thinking about lasagna for dinner. How does that sound?"

She was trying to distract him again. This was what she did. When he tried to convince her to be real with him, she distracted him with sex and food. Anything except to talk to him. "How did he die?"

She shook her head. "I don't want to talk about this. Come on. Can't we just have a nice afternoon? You're right. We have to work tonight. We have to go in and get it done. So let's go upstairs and just relax until we have to go to the club."

"What are you hiding from me?" He was sick of waiting, sick of hoping she would open up to him. He needed the truth. He couldn't stand this. It was like walking through uncharted territory and never knowing when quicksand would swallow him up.

"I'm not hiding anything."

He leaned forward. "I think you are."

She pushed her finger against his chest. "Good for you, Derek. Hey, guess what? You're a fucking cop. Maybe you should do what cops do and investigate."

This wasn't working. When he put her in a corner, she just fought and kicked and scratched. He needed her to talk, needed her to want to tell him. He softened his tone, his stance. He crowded her a little, but not in an aggressive way. Maybe she would respond to his honesty. "Tell me about him, Karina. Tell me your secrets. How bad could it be? Alex told me I need to see you, but how can I do that if you hide from me? This is not how this relationship is supposed to work. We're supposed to be honest with each other."

And he'd given her that. He'd really talked to her. She might not have liked everything she heard, but he'd opened up. He'd talked about his past. He'd talked about what he wanted for his future.

He leaned over and kissed her forehead. "Please, baby. Talk to me."

"Don't call me that."

His jaw tightened. He'd forgotten she didn't like to be called baby, but now he had to wonder why. "Because he called you that? I can't call you baby because you were his baby?"

Tears glistened in her eyes, but she didn't shed them. "I don't know."

His hands came up, gentle as he pushed back her hair. "I don't know if you won't talk to me about him because you loved him too much or because you didn't love him at all. I've stayed away from this because I would rather hear the story from you. Do you know how hard that's been for me? I didn't even know the reason you weren't married anymore. I thought you were divorced. I didn't know why the marriage broke up. Just tell me about him."

"I married him. He died. What the hell else do you need to know?"

He dropped his hands, utterly at a loss as to how to deal with her. "Fine. You're not my baby. You don't want to talk about your husband. I've got that down now. Let's talk about what you did before you came to Texas. Were you always a PI? Is that e-mail account associated with work you did in New York?"

He'd tried to be gentle with her, tried to be intimate, and she'd shoved him back as hard as she could. The least she could do was talk about the goddamn job.

"No." She hesitated, seeming to want to say more, her hand starting to reach out to him, but she dropped it again. "That particular account didn't have anything to do with work. That account was one I had when I was in college. I got married young and I went to school. I went to Brooklyn College. Sociology degree."

It surprised him, but he could see it now. Now that he'd spent time with Karina, he could see her doing social work. "How would he have known about that account, Karina?"

He would be careful. Perhaps it was time to pull back, to treat her with a professional distance. He leaned against the car next to her, but careful to keep himself apart. He couldn't do this dance again. He'd been right in the first place. He needed a sub who needed him, who brought him some modicum of peace, not a woman who made him feel like he'd gotten kicked in the gut every time he looked at her.

"I don't know how he found out about it." Her voice had gone quiet and it took everything he had not to reach out and haul her close, but he'd attempted affection and it hadn't worked. "The address had my name in it. Maybe he got lucky."

"I don't like it." Something was off. "He didn't send e-mails to the other women." Not victims. He wouldn't call them victims because he couldn't put Karina in that group. No matter what she did, he couldn't imagine her gone.

"He's evolving. He's becoming more intimate with his victims." Karina didn't seem to notice that the word made him wince. "He might be getting frustrated because I changed my habits. He's having to learn them all over again. I'm sure I was a much easier target before you moved in with me. Maybe we should think about that."

He huffed a little. "Now I'm supposed to leave you alone? I ask a couple of questions and you want to kick me out?"

"You're not behaving in a professional manner, Derek. Think about this for a second. If he decides I'm too hard a target, he's going to kill someone else. Can you live with that?"

"Fuck, yeah, I can live with that." He knew it was wrong, but if it was Karina or someone else, he would pick someone else. Anyone else.

"I don't understand you." Karina got in his space, her anger obvious. "Maybe you can but I can't. So if you can't treat me with some professional courtesy, maybe you should be reassigned."

Was he really having it out in a parking lot? He wasn't this guy. He was the calm guy who talked shit out. He did not throw down with his sub in a fucking parking lot, except Karina seemed to bring out the worst in him. "I would love to see you try, sweetheart."

"You don't think I can? You don't think I can get you booted right off this case?"

Anger, jealousy, all the nasty emotions he'd had churning in his gut, flashed through him. "You go ahead and make that call. Who are you going to bring in? You going to bring in O'Donnell? Maybe he can fuck you for a while since Tag's out of town. Or hell, maybe you haven't fucked Little Tag in too long. Their wives don't seem to give a damn. Give you something to do. I know how much you need it."

Her hand cracked across his face, damn near twisting his head around because Karina didn't do the polite, lady-slap thing. No, when his baby got pissed she punched and hard. And he deserved it because he'd been way out of line. Even as the words had come out of his mouth, he'd known they were wrong.

Her eyes widened and she stepped back. "Derek, I'm so sorry. I don't know why I did that."

He knew exactly why she'd done it. "Because I inferred you were sleeping with a married man?"

She nodded and backed away, her eyes shifting to the ground. Her breath came out in little panicked pants. "Yeah, the whore thing kind of gets to me. I really hate that."

So Alex was right and he was a douchebag dickwad with infidelity issues. No woman looked that shocked when they had actually done the crime. She made him so crazy. "I didn't say you were a whore, Karina. I didn't even think that. I was just being a jealous idiot."

"No, you just thought I was sleeping with my friends' husbands." She'd gone a nice shade of white and he would have done anything, anything to have kept his mouth shut.

"I'm sorry. God knows I've probably had far more meaningless sex than you have. It wasn't fair or right for me to say something like that." And he had to stop thinking that way. She wasn't Maia. She didn't deserve to pay for Maia's crimes. "Baby, let's go inside."

She shook her head, stepping back from him again, hitting against the side of the car. "No."

"I called you baby. I'm sorry." He had to fix this. He'd made a fucking mess of it. He'd just told himself it would be best to move away from her and the instant he had a real chance to do it, he panicked. He didn't want to leave her. He couldn't trust her to anyone else. "I don't call you baby."

Something had happened to her. Her hands were shaking. He grabbed them, holding them between his. He deepened his voice because she needed something to hold on to. He needed to ground her. He'd done this to her and he had to make it right. "Karina, calm down. Listen to my voice and calm down. Let's go home. I've got my kit upstairs. I'll tie you up and you'll feel safe and I swear I won't ask another question. You have my word on it. I won't call you baby and I won't ask you anything about your past."

"I don't want to talk about it." Her teeth were chattering like she was cold.

"You don't have to. You don't ever have to tell me." He knew that look. She was scared. He'd put her in a bad place and that was the last thing he wanted to do.

This was why she needed to play. It wasn't play at all for her. It was therapy. Some people hit the gym when the stress got to be too much. Some people drank. Some did worse. Karina played. She let the pain and the discipline center her.

"Let me take care of you." He could give it back to her. He could spend an hour with her, giving her what she needed and then they could talk. He would talk at least. He would let her know that her secrets were her own and he wouldn't pry again.

She looked up at him, her eyes a little wide, and he felt her start to relax.

"Karina, is this guy bugging you?"

He turned and saw a man standing at the hood of the car, a frown on his face. He was dressed in sweats and a long-sleeved T-shirt despite the heat. He was sweating and his eyes were on Karina. Derek moved in front of her, putting his body in the way. He could easily make it to his gun if he needed to. "Who are you?"

Karina moved from behind him. "He's my brother-in-law, Derek. Hi, Terry. How are you?"

"Did this asshole make you cry?" Terry pointed a finger at Derek. That was when he noticed the bright blue cast around his hand. It looked like it went all the way up to his elbow. "Is this one of those perverts? I told you to stay away from that shit."

Derek was just about to take care of him because the last thing Karina needed was another fight. She needed to be calm.

"Terry, please. Can we go upstairs to my place?" Karina turned to Derek. "He was Kevin's brother. Why don't you go pick up dinner for us or something?"

"I'll keep my mouth shut, but I'm not leaving you alone." Not for anything. Not even to make her happy. He'd been a fuckwad asshole and she might never forgive him, but he wasn't leaving her alone if he didn't absolutely have to.

Karina frowned and turned away, seemingly in control again and obviously unhappy with him. She started talking to her brother-in-law and Derek had to wonder if he hadn't just ruined everything.

\* \* \* \*

"How are you feeling? When are you going to get that cast off?" Karina shut the door behind her, totally aware that Derek's eyes were watching her every move. She tried to focus on Terry.

Terry sat down at her bar, glancing around to see where Derek had gone. "Does he really have to be here?"

"Where else would I go? I live here." Derek was a grim-faced guardian who seemed intent on destroying her.

"What?" Terry turned to her, shaking his head. "You said this was casual."

If she hadn't promised Liam, she would have told Terry everything. She would have thrown Derek right under a damn bus, then stopped the bus, backed over him and hit him again.

He thought the worst of her. He thought she'd slept with every man at Sanctum apparently. Hypocrite.

And yet when he'd held her hands and promised to make everything better, she'd wanted to go with him so badly. She'd wanted to nod and let him pick her up because she'd believed him. She'd believed he would give her what she'd needed. He would make her safe and she could fight her urges. She'd known if she just gave over to Derek, she wouldn't even think about using.

Thank god for Terry. She could talk to him and then ditch Derek and find a meeting. She would do it tonight at some point. She could handle it. She didn't need him. She was in control, and if he thought for one second she was sleeping with him again, he was so wrong.

"He's sleeping on the couch while his apartment is being

fumigated." Derek would never live in a place that needed to be fumigated. She was already thinking about how to get him back. How did one get revenge on the clean freak who called his lover a whore? She wondered where she could get a dozen rats.

His lips curled up slightly. Damn, the man was sexy. Why did he have to be so awful? "Really, you're going with that? All right. I'm sleeping on the couch because my place is horribly messy and needs fumigation."

Asshole. "So you didn't answer my question, Terry. How's the arm?"

Terry turned back to her, holding up his bad arm. "Healing up but it's going to be weeks until I can use it again. I just came from the doctor's. I thought I would check in on you. I haven't seen you at all this week. You have a busy life."

Somehow he could make innocuous words seem salacious. "Not usually. I've just been working."

"I haven't seen your office yet." He put his hands on the counter, relaxing back. "I think Kevin would be proud that you're out on your own working."

"He taught me everything I know." Her hands were still shaking slightly. Derek had pushed her. When she got that into a corner, she struggled to handle it. She couldn't break down in front of him. Maybe he thought she was a whore, but at least she was a strong one.

She needed something to do. She started making coffee. It was going to be a long night.

"Hey, has that package come in?" Terry asked.

She turned on the faucet. For once her sink was clean. Really clean. So was the coffee pot. It made her life so much easier. And she could find things, like the note from the office she'd gotten yesterday. She'd forgotten about it because Derek had shoved her over the bar and spread her legs wide. "Yes, but I'm going to have to get it tomorrow. It's after five and the manager's office is closed."

Derek frowned. "I thought the office closed at six every day."

"Saturday is early bird special at the diner. She closes up at five." She opened the cabinet, praying she had some coffee left, but she should have known. Derek had two cans in a neat line along with the filters and sugar. Such a freak.

A freak who had a wife who had cheated on him. Many times. How had that affected him? And it wasn't like she'd told him anything. Every time he asked about her friendships with the guys, she'd deflected. Now she could see he'd tried to talk to her about it. And there were plenty of lifestylers she knew who didn't have a problem with casual sex, even after marriage. None of them were at Sanctum, but it was very likely Derek knew some.

He was jealous. Blindingly jealous. What the hell was she supposed to do with that? She'd expected him to be distant with her. He hadn't been that. He'd gotten close. He'd been open.

"I'm going to talk to the manager about that. And the security in the building. And the downstairs bathroom." He moved to the bar. "Do you want me to go and talk someone into getting your package?"

He shouldn't be allowed to be sweet. Jerk. He made her mad, but then maybe that was what people in love did.

Damn it. She couldn't be in love with Derek Brighton. She just couldn't.

Terry put his good hand up. "No, no. Karina, don't go to any bother. I was just curious. I was in the neighborhood."

She sighed. She'd promised him she'd look out for the package and then she'd kind of avoided it. Guilt bit her again, a feeling in the pit of her stomach. Kevin's things were in that package. Kevin had saved her. Kevin had loved her. Shouldn't she be waiting for anything that belonged to him? But no, she was busy in bed with Derek Brighton, who accused her of sleeping around. Who cleaned her apartment and brought her coffee every morning. Who rubbed her feet and then sucked on her toes until she laughed and tried to wriggle away from him.

She'd started out comparing the men because she'd thought Derek would pale. Derek took care of her. Kevin's version of D/s had been different. He'd been older than her and he'd had expectations of a wife. He would never have made her a deal that she cooked and he cleaned. He made the money and she took care of the house. It had been good for her at the time. She'd been happy, but now she wondered if she would have stayed that way or if they would have fought as she found her career. Maybe they would have grown together, but she wondered.

Her love for Kevin had been a combination of hero worship and a young girl's love. He'd been her savior, her father figure, her mentor, her lover.

Derek had somehow become her friend. Derek had somehow become her partner, despite the fact that he had serious issues.

So did she. What if they could work it out?

"Karina? Are you okay?" Terry was staring at her.

Derek was, too, but he looked more curious than worried.

"I'm fine." She shook off her worries. It would do no good to dwell on them. She couldn't figure anything out tonight. She needed to let it go or she would end up in a bad place. She needed to get through the night at the club with Derek and then she could ask Li to take her to a meeting. She would let Derek believe anything he liked.

Or she could try to talk to him. She could see if he could understand.

Terry slapped the counter. "You're more than fine, sweetheart. You're great." He stood up and gave her a long look. "I have to get out of here. I'm meeting a friend for dinner. You probably won't be able to get that package until Monday."

He was right about that. "Sunday is the manager's day off. I'll pick it up Monday morning."

"Then maybe we can have dinner Monday night." Terry walked around the bar and gave her a hug. "It would be good to catch up. If you're not doing anything, of course."

"Absolutely." There was something odd about holding him. Maybe he was thinner than he used to be, but something about his arms around her felt off. She couldn't put her finger on it. It didn't matter. Just being around Terry made her feel guilty. Made her worry she didn't think enough about the family that had helped her.

He stepped back and nodded. He frowned Derek's way and then made his way to the door, opening it with his right hand and leaving.

And she was alone with Derek.

She stopped, afraid to turn around because she didn't want to start the fight again. She couldn't go back into this with him. Not tonight. She needed calm.

His hands came on her shoulders. "So you talked about lasagna?"

"Yeah."

She felt him kiss her hair. "That sounds great."

He stepped away and then she heard the TV come on and when she turned, he was sitting down and a baseball game was on. He sat down but even from where she stood she could see the tension in his shoulders.

They were both wary, both hurt. She'd been hurt by his words and he'd been hurt because she wouldn't talk.

They had hours to get through before they were supposed to take on their roles, but maybe they didn't need to wait. He'd offered to top her. She didn't want to play anymore. She wanted something softer.

She had a choice to make. She could rail at him or she could take the peace he was offering.

Karina left the kitchen and walked to her temporary Dom, to the man she was pretty certain she would mourn as surely as she mourned her husband.

He looked up at her. "Ba…Karina, it's all right. I'm not going to push you. You're safe."

She was safe because she was with him. She sank to her knees and let her head rest on his lap. "Can we order pizza? I would rather sit with you."

His hand was in her hair, smoothing it, petting her. "Yes, of course."

She listened as he called their order in. It was all right. Derek would take care of things. For now.

That was all that mattered anyway.

# Chapter Ten

Derek didn't like the way Master Will looked at Karina. Of course, he didn't like the way any of them looked at Karina, but he had to get a freaking handle on that. They looked at her because she was gorgeous and wearing very little clothing. He stared at her as she stood at the bar, getting them both drinks. There wouldn't be a lick of alcohol in them. They were working. He could use a beer, but he suspected he was going to cut back heavily on his drinking.

He was going to change a lot of things because nothing, nothing in the world had ever felt as good as that moment when Karina sank to her knees and laid her head on his lap. Nothing. No sex, no triumph, no promotion had ever made him as peaceful, as complete as having her trust him.

One day she would tell him what he already suspected, but if she never did, he would be content with the Karina he had now. He'd seen her, really seen her, and that was all he needed.

"Are you going to kill the doc?" Sean stood beside him, his blue eyes wary as he looked across the room to where Karina was waiting on the other bartender to finish their drinks.

"Only if I have to." He wasn't sure about the doc. He'd read through the files Liam had sent him as Karina and he had eaten a quiet dinner. Will Daley was a liar, but was he a killer? "What does Eve say about him?"

"Adam hacked into the hospital network and got some of the depositions about his upcoming trial."

"Do any of you understand the words 'usable' and 'evidence'?" They were going to kill him. He might catch the guy, but McKay-Taggart's highly suspect investigative techniques would put him right back out on the street.

Sean shrugged. "If he gets off on a technicality, we'll let Jesse kill him. Jesse hasn't killed anyone in a while. He needs to let off a little pressure."

Derek turned to him. Sometimes he couldn't tell when they were joking. The last thing he needed was another dead body. "Are you serious?"

Sean held a hand up. "Chill. I promise we'll figure out a way to do this by the book when you arrest him, but for now we need a break. We need to know where to look. As far as I can tell the doc over there has been seen at all three clubs where the victims played. I think he's definitely a person of interest. He might have been just trying to find the right club or the lawsuit was the inciting incident that set him off. Eve's going over all the files tonight. She wants to see how he behaved during the deposition. She couldn't do it earlier because she and Alex were meeting with the adoption agency, but she swears she'll get to it tonight. I also got the info you asked me about."

Alex and Eve were adopting? That was nice. Maybe a passel of babies would calm the group down. Or just start another generation of evil geniuses. Did Karina want babies? His parents were always on him about grandkids. He wasn't getting any younger.

"Derek?"

"Sorry."

Sean shook his head. "I know that look, man. Just give in."

He wasn't about to argue with Sean. He kind of already had given in. He could tell himself it was best to distance from Karina but he flat out didn't want to. He wasn't going to lie to himself anymore. He wanted her. He didn't want some unknown sub who would mindlessly obey him. He wanted Karina and she needed him. She didn't need a part-time play partner. She needed a Dom. Hell, she needed a husband who protected her, who loved her.

"I don't know if she'll let me in. I fucked up earlier today. We're fine right now, but she's probably counting the hours until she can kick me out." Master Will and his sub moved to the bar. Fucker. Still, if he rushed over it would look weird. He had to stay calm. Trust Karina. Trust the team.

"Tell me you didn't accuse her of sleeping around."

He winced a little. "I would love to tell you that, but my mother taught me not to lie."

Sean groaned. "Dumbass. Karina isn't Maia."

He stared at her as she smiled up at Master Will. Now that he was really looking at her, the real Karina and not the one he'd made up in his head, he could see the difference in her smile. She was giving

Master Will her best "client" smile. Pretty, friendly and warm, but without the all-out glow she saved for her friends. And without the heat she reserved for him. "I know. Not even close. If it makes you feel better, I accused her of sleeping with you as well as O'Donnell and the big guy. She didn't give me enough time or I would have thrown the Brit in."

He was such a fucking dumbass and he had to pray Karina could forgive him.

Sean had a great poker face. His expression never changed. "Don't you ever tell the women. Ever."

Shit. He hadn't thought about the ramifications. "You think they would be mean to Karina?"

Sean huffed and rolled his eyes. "No, they love Karina. They will be more than mean to you. They will take off your balls and do crafts with them or some shit. You do not want to piss off the subs. Seriously. They've unionized. We should never have let them start that book club."

The idea of the Sanctum subs looking for a little revenge spooked him. He didn't want to know what Charlotte would do to him. "Yeah, let's keep my stupidity between us. Do you think it would help my case if I ask her to marry me?"

Sean's poker face dropped away. "Are you fucking kidding me?"

"I don't think she'll say yes." He'd thought he'd never get married again. He thought he'd control the relationship by keeping it to a contracted D/s partnership with securely placed boundaries.

He didn't want boundaries between them. He didn't want fucking walls. He just wanted her. He wanted his wife. He wanted to take her home and have his mom fuss over her and his dad tell her she was far too good for his son. He wanted to get dragged to church and sit beside her and hold her hand.

"Well, then we'll have to set the subs on her," Sean said with an evil grin. "A few casually placed words about how she broke your heart and they'll be all over her. They love drama and more than that they love matchmaking. I would be utterly terrified if I wasn't married to the ringleader. Grace believes it's her mission in life to make sure everyone gets married. I think she's getting kickbacks from a wedding planner."

At least he had an appeals board. He kept his eyes steady on Karina. She seemed a little concerned. Master Will shook his head and ran a hand over his brow before nodding and stepping away. He felt better when both Master Will and his sub walked away. "So did you run a background check on the brother-in-law? I don't like him."

"I didn't like him either," Sean agreed. "He pushed her to feel bad about dating. It's been years since her husband was killed in the line of duty. He was NYPD."

Shit. Would she marry another cop? He was mostly behind a desk at this point in his career, but there were always risks with his job. He wanted to know the story so badly, but he stopped himself. That was Karina's story to tell, and he would hear it from her or not at all. "So what's the line on Terry Mills?"

"He's drifted a lot. His mother died before his brother. The father was killed in a boating accident when Terry was sixteen. The family made their money off the dad's business. He had a boat and gave tourists tours of Long Island Sound. Kevin became a cop in the city, but Terry took the boat and kept up the business after he turned eighteen. After Kevin died, he took the boat to the Caribbean and had been working there until he showed up in Dallas a couple of months back."

Derek frowned. "I thought he'd only been here for a few weeks?"

Sean shrugged. "He told Karina he came to rehab his broken arm. I guess it was worse than he said."

"A broken arm heals in six to eight weeks. I've had more than one broken bone."

Sean shook his head. "Look, I don't like the guy, either, but we're looking for a serial killer."

"He would have known her e-mail. He might think that's still her e-mail." His brain was working overtime. Yes, they were looking for a serial killer, but what if they were being manipulated? What if they were seeing what the killer wanted them to see?

Sean's eyes widened. "I'm going to call Adam. I'll have him check into some things. Do we know the doctor he's been seeing?"

He shook his head. "Find out and keep it quiet because Karina doesn't need to know anything until we're sure." It would kill her. It would threaten her calm and he wasn't going to do that again unless he had to. "And see if we can put a tail on him. I'm going to make sure Karina isn't alone with the man again, and I think I need to break into her apartment manager's office. That shouldn't be hard."

"Fun. Why?"

"He's very interested in a package she's supposed to get."

Sean's eyes narrowed. "He mentioned it the first day. I'll get on it and we'll find out where he's staying and tail him for a couple of days."

"Good." He didn't like the coincidence. He'd been a cop long enough that he knew coincidence was just a word people used. Coincidence usually meant something shitty was about to happen.

He didn't like the fact that her brother-in-law had shown up and suddenly someone had her name on a grain of rice and that meant death. Yeah, one plus one equaled two, and that usually meant that money was involved.

Money was involved far more often than psychosis. Most people with hormonal challenges got help and never hurt a person. People who were greedy on the other hand…

Karina walked his way. God, she was gorgeous. His Gorgeous Girl. His. Fucking his. She wouldn't stray. She wouldn't look another way. She would take all that love and lust and send it his way if he was lucky. She would take that sexy feminine energy and spend it on the man who brought her comfort and pleasure and who made her feel loved.

He was going to be that man. He was going to be that man if it killed him.

"Hey, I got you a rum and Coke." She smiled his way and winked to let him know it was just a Coke. Hers would be the same.

He kind of thought hers would be the same for a different reason. How did he tell her that it was okay? How did he tell her he didn't give a fuck? Would she even believe a damn word he said at this point?

There was only one reason he could think of if she had a record. Karina Mills wouldn't harm another person. Karina wouldn't commit armed robbery or even shoplift.

But if her life was bad, she might hurt herself. She might have taken drugs to escape when she was young.

And he knew damn well she would pull herself up and fix the problem because that was the kind of woman she was. She was strong and brave and so fucking gorgeous it hurt to look at her.

She was everything a man could want.

"Thanks, gorgeous." It hurt to not call her what she was. He knew it was dumb, but she was his baby. He'd never called Maia that. When he was young, it was because that was what his dad called his mom. As he'd gotten older, he'd realized that Maia wasn't his baby.

Karina was his baby. He might never say it, but it was true. She was the one.

He'd been a dumbshit asshole, but she was the one.

She smiled Sean's way. Again, a very pretty smile, but not the one reserved for her lover. He was her lover and he was going to do whatever it took to make sure it stayed that way.

He took his Coke and maneuvered his way next to her. "Thanks, gorgeous. What did Master Will want?"

"He's not feeling well. He just came over to tell me he and Starr are heading home. He wanted to make sure I was okay." She took a sip and smiled his way.

God, how did he tell her he loved her? He'd fucked this up on a fundamental level. She had to think he wouldn't accept her. He hated she thought so little of him.

He looked at the clock. It was past one. The club would be open for a little bit more, but they were past the heavy scenes. He'd avoided them tonight. If he'd been at Sanctum, he would have stripped her down and flogged her. He would have tied her to a cross and laid into her, but he didn't trust the eyes on her here. At Sanctum they would honor his claim. The minute he got a real collar around her throat the men would praise her beauty, but no one would make a move on her. They would honor her for the gorgeous submissive she was.

Here, he worried they would simply take her. Without love. Without honor. Without thought to who she really was. Gorgeous. Smart. So fucking strong she brought him to his knees.

"Are you ready to go?" He wanted to get her out of here. He wouldn't feel good until he had her back at his place, behind locked doors and in his bed. He'd long ago learned to trust his instincts and they were telling him it was time to stop. Karina didn't know it, but she was going to his place tonight.

"If you think it's the right time, then yes." Karina nodded his way, obviously giving in.

She wanted to stay and if he thought for a second it was in her best interest, in her interest in any way, he would likely turn it around. It wasn't. None of this was. He was going to tell the Rangers tomorrow to fuck themselves and he and Karina were going on a vacation. He would give them every lead he had, but his girl was out of this. Nothing was worth her safety. She was the most precious thing in the world to him. If he lost his job, then Ian fucking Taggart better get ready for a new employee.

He was putting Karina first.

"Go and change your clothes. Don't take long and don't bother with a shower. I'll just get you dirty again." He couldn't walk out and get into the car with her in a corset and thong. Though it should be legal because she was so pretty.

She glanced Sean's way and her bratty beautiful eyes rolled. "He's going to kill me, Sean. I'll see you both back here in ten."

She sashayed her way toward the locker room. God, he wasn't going to let that go. Her ass was the prettiest thing he'd ever seen.

And she needed him. She needed him to center her. She needed him so she didn't devolve into chaos and dirt. God only knew her bathroom needed him.

He would move her into his place. Better yet, he would let her pick a place and then properly organize their stuff and hire a maid. She would cook and he would handle the daily cleaning.

They would be happy.

"Dude, you're in too deep," Sean said.

He shrugged. "I don't want to be anything else."

"Then I apologize. You're in just deep enough."

He could happily drown if she would just keep smiling his way.

\* \* \* \*

Karina stepped into the hallway that led to the locker room. She kind of hated Kink. Loved the word. Hated the club because it didn't take itself seriously. There was a long corridor that led to the only private place in the club. There were two doors that opened off but she wasn't sure where they led. It was stupid, but she felt a little vulnerable as she passed them.

They didn't open. She walked on. The lights flickered above her, casting shadows on the hallway. She turned and she could see Liam standing at the beginning of the hall. He'd been at the front door, but she was certain Derek had called him over.

If she let him, she was sure Derek would charge into the bathroom and stand guard over her.

She pushed through the door that led to the women's locker room. At least it was well lit. It closed behind her and she was alone. She let out a deep breath. She hadn't been alone in days. Even when they were here at the club, they tended to leave when it closed so all the subs were changing at the same time. It was deserted now. Peaceful. Quiet.

What the hell was she going to do about Derek?

She heard a shower turn on. So much for being alone. In and out. She would change clothes and get right back to Derek. She would run his way. Maybe they could keep up this sweet peace they had found between them. She could forgive his stupidity. He was bruised, damaged by what had happened to him. She could understand that. He'd been sweet since the moment he'd realized he was wrong. Karina believed in second chances.

He accepted her silence. She had no doubt he would take her home and make love to her and hold her. So why was there a lump in her throat?

It was probably because she knew her time with him was almost up. A few weeks. Nothing more. They would solve the case or dissolve the task force. They wouldn't let him stay forever.

He wouldn't let himself stay forever. He would go looking for his sweet sub who would never question him. She shouldn't. She should be smarter than Karina. Derek did right. He only ever veered off the path for someone he cared about. When he loved someone, he would do anything to protect her.

She didn't deserve that.

Her heels clacked along the floor as she made her way to the line of lockers. What was she doing? She wanted Derek. She couldn't imagine going forward without him, but she was holding back. He'd been so sweet all afternoon. He'd given in on everything. He'd told her she could have her way and perversely it made her want to open up to him.

She found her locker and opened it with a sigh. She needed to go to a meeting. She needed to sit and drink craptastic coffee and tell her story. She needed to walk in there and know she would be accepted for exactly who she was. She needed to know she could walk on her own two feet with her head held high. No one was ever waiting for her. Kevin thought she should do it alone to be strong.

Would Derek wait for her? She kind of thought that if Derek could accept her, he would sit outside the meeting. If he was her husband, he would escort her to and from and hold her hand. He would tell her to do what she needed and that when she was done, he would be there. It was a part of who he was.

It wasn't a betrayal. It was just a difference. She'd needed Kevin. She'd needed exactly what he'd given her at the time. She hadn't been ready for the kind of real intimacy she'd found with Derek. She'd needed the boundaries Kevin had given her. He'd loved her in his way. He'd shown her a lifestyle that helped her and given her the kind of distant affection she'd been able to accept at the time. If he'd been as attentive as Derek, she likely would have been wary, would have run away again.

Now she needed to tease Derek and lie in bed with him like a lazy slug and have him bring her coffee. She needed to laugh when he tickled her and she needed to wake him up when his dreams got bad.

She needed to love Derek. She needed to be loved by him.

God, what would she do if he walked away?

There was a sound from the showers that caught her attention. She turned, worried suddenly.

Master Will walked out of the showers, his face pale, his hands reaching for her. "Karina."

He shouldn't be here. Oh, fuck. She stepped back. She wasn't carrying, but she could still handle herself. "You stay back."

She noticed there was a smear of dirty reddish brown on the doorway as he lumbered through. She could see the blood he'd left where he'd placed his hand.

"Karina..." He stomped toward her, but there was something wrong with him. He moved without grace, as though forcing himself along. "Run, Karina."

She didn't need any more prompting. She started to turn and that was when she felt something sharp against her shoulder. There was a burning sensation and she swatted her hand back, but her vision was already odd.

Slow. She was slowing down.

Starr stood in front of her, a needle in her hand. "I am going to be so glad when I don't have to come to these places anymore. You're all sick, you know. Terry, we should hurry. Are you sure the bin is big enough?"

"I'm sure, baby doll. I got this planned out down to the last detail. You just trust me." The last thing she saw before the darkness closed in on her was her brother-in-law's face sneering down.

Derek was going to be so mad at her...

# Chapter Eleven

Derek looked down the hallway, staring where Karina had disappeared. The men's locker room was on the opposite side of the building, but he'd left Liam watching her while he'd picked up his stuff and changed into street clothes. She was taking her sweet time. As long as he was waiting, it might be good to do some damage control. "How's it going, O'Donnell?"

The Irishman's brows rose. "Careful there, Brighton. I might think you're being friendly."

"I'm sorry, man." He was about to go into a major explanation because O'Donnell was Karina's friend and he needed to start playing nicely with Karina's friends. "I can only..."

O'Donnell held a hand up. "I've met your ex-wife. I understand. Just treat Karina well and we'll be all right, you and me. You talked to Sean? He told you what we found out about Terry Mills?"

"I'd like to know what doctor he's seeing." He couldn't get his mind off the brother-in-law. Something had been off about him earlier.

"I'll have Adam try to get his medical records. Do you think he's faking the broken arm? Why would he do that? Is he trying to get sympathy from Karina?"

Derek could think of only a couple of reasons, but his mind was working overtime. "I need to get her to talk to me about her marriage. I'm not trying to pry, but I don't like the fact that her brother-in-law walked in just as Karina is being threatened. Do you know anything? Were they close? Would he want revenge on her for some reason?"

O'Donnell whistled. "Damn me. You think he's the one who's after her. He's been in town longer than he admitted to Karina. He's lying about that. Who knows what else he could be lying about?"

"I don't know, but he's a ship captain. He's going to be good with ropes." His mind turned. Plug and play. Take a suspect and answer the questions. He had the who and how and the when. This was tricky because there didn't seem to be a why, but money was always bubbling right under the surface. "Did the brother have any property of value? Karina obviously didn't keep it. The mother died before Karina's husband. Was the will left in probate? Sometimes it can take years." Maybe Terry didn't think Karina deserved anything. Or maybe there was something else he was missing.

He needed to figure out what was in that box.

"No idea, but I'll find out. Adam can run a search on the whole family. Karina's husband was killed in a drug related shootout. As far as I can tell, he was a good cop. There was nothing dirty about him. He was posthumously honored as a hero, but things aren't always as they seem." Liam looked down the hallway.

"Have you been here the whole time?" He didn't like how long Karina was taking.

"I've been standing here the whole time. The only person who's moved around back there was someone taking out the laundry. She pushed one of those carts out the back door. I went back there, but Karina was in the shower. I told her to hurry it up."

His heart started pounding and he turned and started down the hall. He'd told Karina to skip the shower, but Liam didn't know that. Karina wouldn't disobey him. *Shit. Shit. Shit.* It made sense. It would be an easy way to get her out. "How long ago?"

Liam was running beside him. "Five minutes tops. I called out to her in the locker room, but the shower was on. She's fine, Derek."

But he had the sudden feeling that she wasn't. "You didn't see her."

"I can't walk into the ladies' dressing room."

Derek hit the dressing room running. Nothing. It was quiet with the singular exception of a shower running somewhere in the back.

*Please please please please be there. Please be there.*

Liam stopped in front of the lockers. "Shit, is that blood?"

Sure enough, there was a smear of fresh blood on the doorway leading to the lockers.

"Karina!" He didn't give a shit who freaked out that he was in there. He barreled into the shower area and ripped open the plastic curtain.

Nothing but an empty stall.

"Fuck me." Liam pulled his cell. "Sean, get out to the parking lot. He has Karina. He took her out in a laundry bin."

Derek stood there staring at the place where the water hit the tile. She was gone. Taken by a person who had already killed four times. Gone. Right out from under his nose. He was supposed to protect her, defend her, and he'd been changing into jeans while she fought for her life. Panic slowed him, made time seem to stop.

"Lieutenant?"

Who? Where would he take her? Where the hell was she? She should have been safe in his arms, but he'd been arrogant. He'd promised to protect her.

"Lieutenant!" O'Donnell whirled him around. "Snap out of it. I know you're terrified, but she doesn't need her lover right now. She needs the cop. You shove everything you're feeling down and concentrate on the case. Now."

Derek nodded. Li was right. He had to get it together. There were clues and they might, just might lead him to Karina if he could stop freaking out and concentrate.

But first he called an APB in on Karina, Terry Mills, and Will Daley. He didn't give a flying fuck that he was rolling the dice, and if he was wrong they could fire him. It didn't matter. All that mattered was finding Karina before...

Finding Karina. He was going to find Karina.

"You said it was a woman." Liam had seen the person pushing the laundry cart. He'd called that person a she.

"I was standing a good twenty-five feet away, but she was small. I couldn't see her hair, but there was no way that frame was male. She had breasts. I would bet they were fake. I can tell a fake set from a mile away."

The doctor's sub had fake breasts.

"Secure this room. No one gets in or out. I mean no one. This is a crime scene. I'll have a forensic team here in fifteen minutes." He started for the door that led to the hallway. He couldn't be so far behind.

"All right, Lieutenant. Where are you going?"

"I'm going to find out how she took Karina out of here." He was minutes behind her. The question was had the killer been waiting outside? He rather thought not. He would bet his life that the killer had been in the locker room, too. If Starr was in on it, then there was no way she took down Karina on her own. Even if she managed to drug her, that little stick creature couldn't pick her up, couldn't get her into a laundry bin.

How many people had been in that bin? At the very least Karina and the killer had been rolled out.

He turned right and saw the door that led to the loading dock. Using his boot, he kicked it open. He wasn't about to add his fingerprints. The crime scene would already be a nightmare.

Fresh air hit his lungs as he stepped on the dock. There was a ramp that moved down toward the lot. There were four light posts, none of them with working illumination. Most of the visitors parked in the front lot. No one was out here. He turned to his left and there was the damn laundry bin.

Fuck, if she died, he would lie down beside her and never get up. Nothing would matter if he failed her.

He jogged around, looking for anything, anyone. He was in the middle of the city, but it was quiet. Too damn quiet. He could hear the freeway in the distance. He looked around for security cameras, anything that would tell him what car she'd been dumped in. Nothing. They'd placed cameras in front to catch people coming in and out. Because the victims had been at more than one club, they assumed they needed to check members, not employees, so the employee entrances had been left alone. Big mistake.

He pulled his cell and called it in, requesting a forensic team. It was time to come out of the darkness. He had to get everyone he could on finding her before it was too late.

If the killer followed his pattern, he would take her somewhere quiet, play with her for a while. The previous victims had been tied up prior to death. The patterns were intricate, requiring time and space.

He hated the thought of Karina being tortured, but he would take it over her being dead.

He heard a quiet cursing and then the slamming of a door.

Moving as quietly as he could, he turned the corner into the lot on the side of the building.

And then he remembered the doc's car. On the second night they'd been at the club, he'd followed Master Will out to get a look at his ride. The doctor drove a bright red vintage Mustang. He'd thought it was a sweet ride at the time, and now that fucker stuck out like a sore thumb.

And so did the woman who was trying to get the trunk closed.

"Damn it. Damn it." She sniffled, obviously panicking. Even in the low light, he could see it was Starr. She had changed. She was wearing a bland uniform, her hair in a baseball cap. She stood at the back of the car, trying to shove the trunk down. "Stupid old car."

He stopped. Was Karina still in the trunk? Was she even alive?

The trunk lid popped open again and Starr bit back a cry. She shoved it down as far as it would stay and began to reach into her purse.

In the background, he could see Sean starting around the corner.

"Cut her off!" Derek yelled and then sprinted for the suspect.

Starr screamed. He could see her startled eyes and then she turned to run, but he was on her. Derek didn't give a flying fuck that he might hurt her. He tackled her, sending her right to the pavement.

"Check that trunk," Derek called out.

"Let me go!" Starr struggled underneath him. "Let me go. He made me do it. He was going to kill me if I didn't do it. Let me go!"

"What the fuck is going on?" Sean asked as he jogged to the car. The trunk had popped back open.

"Karina's gone."

"Yeah, I got that from Li. You think she did it?" Sean asked as he pulled the trunk fully open.

"I don't have her." The woman under him gasped and her words were spat out as she cried. "He took her. I was just supposed to drive his car. Please don't hurt me. If you just let me up, you can have some of the money. We can work this out."

"It's not Karina, Derek," Sean said. "It's Will Daley and he's alive. Unconscious, but alive."

Because they would need the patsy alive. They would need someone to pin the murders on.

And just like that he figured it out. Four women had died as nothing but a smoke screen for the one the killer really wanted. Terry Mills was damn good at deflection.

"I know where Karina is."

\* \* \* \*

Karina fought her way back to consciousness. The sedative he'd given her made her head throb. She came to, shivering and unable to move her arms. Damn. She could feel the ropes against her skin. He'd been working for a while, it seemed. Cool air hit her flesh and nausea rolled. Naked. She was naked and trussed up in a not pleasant way.

Through the aching in her head, she tried to remember what had happened. Someone had drugged her. Starr. She was going to get so much hell from the guys for letting that happen. She'd been distracted. Will had shown up. He'd told her to run and then she'd seen Terry.

Terry was the monster. Terry was the one who had tied her up. If she didn't get out of here, Terry would be the one who killed her.

How much time had passed?

"Don't even try to move, bitch." His voice was hard, deeper than she remembered, but then he'd hidden a lot from her.

"What are you doing?" She stayed as still as she could, but she could feel ropes around her wrists. He'd bound them tight. Too tight. She couldn't feel her hands. Her shoulders were pulled and twisted. It was a perversion of what Derek did to her. Derek wrapped her up like a work of art. Derek made her feel safe and beautiful, as though it was his arms around her. This had been done to restrict her, to hurt her, to hold her down for the kill. How far had he gotten?

She forced her eyes open. The world was still blurry. Lights. She could see them, but they were like halos, making the rest of the world fuzzy. *Stay calm.* Beyond her head throbbing, she didn't feel a ton of pain.

"What am I doing? I'm dealing with a problem, Karina. You always were a problem." He came into view, his face frowning down at her.

"I don't understand." Her voice was a little slurred, but she was sure of one thing. She had to keep him talking. She had to take stock. Her hands were tied behind her back, but it felt like her legs were still free. From mid-thigh down she seemed to have some movement. She could use that. She just needed to get a little more control back.

Where the hell was she?

"You don't understand that you corrupted my whole family?" He reached down and slapped her across the face. "Wake up, bitch, because I have a few things to say to you before I put you down."

Pain flared, but it did a damn fine job of making her head clear up. *Calm down. Breathe. Think.* She could beat him.

"How did I corrupt Kevin? I loved Kevin." Keep him talking because Derek was looking for her. He wouldn't let hours pass. He would call in the cavalry and figure out where she was. He would be here and she had to be alive when he busted down the door.

"My brother was a hero and you turned him into a freak. Sometimes I'm glad he died because you would have brought him down, you junkie whore. It was bad enough you did all those drugs, but did you have to make him into a freak?"

"He wasn't a freak. He was a good man." And now that she was here, she could see she'd dishonored her former Master by building walls around herself. He might not have been as deeply affectionate as Derek, but he had loved her. He had given her everything he had. Kevin wouldn't want her to mourn him for the rest of her life. He wouldn't want her to hide. He was proud of her. He'd never hidden her past from his family and friends and co-workers because he thought it proved how strong she was.

"He was a good man until he met you. He arrested you. He should have sent you to fucking jail."

He had the first time. Then one night he'd found her huddling in a building where a bunch of homeless kids had taken refuge. The NYPD had busted the entire place, but he'd led her out to his squad car and she'd been shocked when he took her to his house instead. In the morning, he'd taken her to rehab.

*You got one shot at this, kid. You get through this and I'll put you up at my place. I'll make sure you go to school. You don't and I will take you in next time.*

She'd asked him why and he'd told her nothing so beautiful should be allowed to rot and that's what she'd do in jail. He'd told her she'd never gotten a chance, so he would make sure she got one. When she'd gotten out of rehab, he'd been true to his word. He'd gotten her through her GED. He hadn't touched her for two months. He'd given her space to find her footing. She'd had to kiss him the first time.

Kevin would very likely have been friends with Derek. Good men. Good cops. Good Doms.

And they both had shitty brothers.

"He loved me. He helped me and turned me around. He would not want you to do this." How long did she have before he made his move?

"What he wants doesn't matter anymore. He was always the one our parents loved, you know. He was the smart one. He was the one who didn't get into trouble. 'Why can't you be more like Kevin?' That's what I heard all my fucking life. I even told my mother about the shit he was into. I told her that he was a pervert freak who liked to spank women and you know what she said?"

Karina could only guess. Her mother-in-law had been an amazing woman. Tolerant. Loving. Faithful. Karina could have given him a speech about what a true lady his mother had been, but she wanted him to do the talking so she shook her head. "No."

"She told me that if it made him happy, it was okay. It was only okay because she couldn't see how wrong it was. Because she couldn't see that you had brought her precious son low."

"He introduced me to the lifestyle, but I don't think your mother saw it as being low." It was love and it was between them. Her mother-in-law might very well have said anything that brings a couple closer together was perfectly fine.

She was starting to get used to the light again. She could see more of him, and the first thing she noticed was his bright blue cast. "It's a fake."

He smirked a little. "Yeah. Oh, if anyone asks for my X-rays, I can provide them. I really did break it a couple of months back. It was right about the time I found out Kevin had a life insurance policy none of us knew about. I had to dig through some old files to find the access to ma's old bank accounts. Kevin hadn't touched them so there was still ten grand and a safety deposit box. I guess he decided to use it for his papers. One million dollars just sitting there."

At least she knew why he wanted to kill her. A million would likely buy him a shiny new boat. Terry was always complaining that he didn't get a good deal. After their mother had died, she'd left the money to Kevin because Terry had gotten their dad's boat and his business. Kevin hadn't wanted it and she hadn't even thought about it after he died. She hadn't even realized he had another life insurance policy. "It won't work. Derek will investigate."

"Your new pervert boyfriend? He can investigate all he likes. He'll go exactly where I want him to go. He'll end up here at this house and he'll find your body. I'll even make a little call after the scene is set. Well, I'll let my girl call it in. She can call 911 and say she heard you scream or some shit. The police will get where I want them to go."

She knew something he didn't. "What girl?" She sighed. "Starr. Of course. You're going to pin everything on Will Daley."

"Hey, he's the one who got himself into this freaky crap. After Starr tells the cops about how he liked to beat her, they'll believe anything. You know as well as I do that perception is the key to getting a conviction. Kevin taught me that. I knew I had to come down here and handle you because I'm pretty sure there's paperwork in that box Grant sent you. He said there were some files in there. Kevin always kept a second set of records. I couldn't let you find out about the policy. I'm the secondary on Kevin's life insurance, but I'm not on yours at all. Once you got your hands on that money, I wouldn't be able to get it away."

She had to die before she could claim the policy in order for Terry to get the money. She would have very likely claimed it and set up some sort of charity to help at-risk kids. It would have been a worthy way to honor her husband.

She had to give it to him. The cast worked. No one would think he could do this much damage with a broken arm. A cast was easy to fake with nothing more than a sock and sticky gauze bandages. Unless someone touched it, they wouldn't know it wasn't hard. That was what she'd felt when he hugged her. His arm had been soft where she should have felt the cast.

"How do you know Starr?"

He moved down her body. She shivered because she hated the feel of his hands on her. The ropes shifted and she could feel him twisting, making new knots. Her torso was completely frozen, but he hadn't tied her lower legs yet. She just had to wait for the right time. "She's from the neighborhood. I went to school with her. Caught back up when she worked on a boat I was sailing for some rich guy. She's the one I broke my arm over. She came back to New York with me and we hatched this plan to get the money. She got a job at the therapist's office so if the cops look, they'll find records of me coming in every couple of days. She also found the Daley guy. He's perfect. He's got a whole hidden life. He lies to everyone in his circle. He's perfectly set up. I can see it now. 'But he seemed so normal.' Yeah, that's how all serial killers seem. They're going to find your body in his house and his system full of drugs. He got high. He got violent. He got sloppy. That's the only way to catch serials. By the time his trial starts, my girl and I will have a sweet new boat and we'll be in St. Lucia, far away from here."

"You left Will alive?" She felt bad for the doc. He'd been trying to explore his nature and it had gotten him in trouble, maybe dead.

He shrugged a little. "Sure. It's better to have him alive and protesting. He won't remember a thing and I made sure he doesn't have an alibi for the other girls I did. You know that was the funniest thing of all. I thought I would hate it. I thought that killing those other girls was just smart. I thought I would tie them up and shoot them, but when I looked into that first girl's eyes, I wanted my hands on her. I wanted her to know it was me killing her, judging her. And somehow, she became you, dear sister. She morphed into you."

He'd gone way off the deep end. "This is not going down the way you want it to."

He adjusted the ropes and pulled out his cell, frowning at it.

"She's supposed to be here, isn't she?" Karina walked through the plan. Maybe Starr was in another room, but then why would he keep glancing back at the door, checking his phone. Someone had to get Will's car home. They wouldn't risk coming together. If Starr got pulled over, she could claim her boyfriend was just drunk. She couldn't get away with two bodies.

So she was missing in action. More time for Karina.

"It won't work if he's not here. You have to time this just right, Terry. If you're even a little bit off, the cops are going to figure it out."

His jaw tightened and he stood back up, looking out the window. "No. They won't even bother. I'm handing them a great case. The cops will run with it. They'll look like heroes for stopping this guy at five. I've taken little trophies from each girl and Starr hid them here. They'll also find the rice. I thought that was pretty funny. She used to work at an amusement park. She ran a booth where she wrote people's names on grains of rice. The stupid fuckers still haven't found them. I laid out everything."

It might have actually worked, except there was no way Derek let the little things slip. Maybe it was time to disrupt Terry's calm. She needed him close. She didn't need her hands to hurt him. She just needed to get her feet close enough.

"They found the rice, Terry. Why do you think Lieutenant Brighton has been living with me? He moved in the day after they found Amanda King's body. He isn't my boyfriend. He's a cop and he's looking for me right this second. There's no way he buys this."

He stared down at her. "No."

"Yes. You watched me before. Did I have men over?"

"You went to that club all the time. It had too much security. I had to get you to go somewhere else. I met the mom of that girl. She told me she was worried about her daughter because she was into freaky stuff. That was when I came up with my plan."

Oh, god, she'd been the reason for Tanya's death. "I'm sure after she was killed, you were the one who sent her to me."

"I did. I had to get you on the outside. I don't care if your friend is a cop. He's still going to see what I want him to see. Hell, I'll even give him a call in the morning and he can tell me the sad news of my sister-in-law's death. I'll cry and shit and tell him I always knew you would come to a bad end. I always knew those clubs would be the death of you. Once I tell him about your background, he won't question it. No one gives a shit about addicts, Karina. I'll tell him about the arrests and what a piece of shit you were as a kid and he'll shrug and probably think the world is better off." He hissed through his teeth as he looked at his phone again. "Fuck this. I'm not waiting."

"You need that car parked in his drive." Karina thought through the situation quickly. Anything to keep his hands off her throat. "We're in the city. Someone's going to notice when his car gets here. You can't go until she's here. Think about it, Terry. What if she broke down? It could be hours. How do you explain that his car got here after my time of death? They can tell. You know that."

He kicked her right in the gut. Karina moaned, but it was better than getting strangled to death.

He turned away.

*Think.* She looked around as much as she could. Will Daley's house was neat and uncluttered. Damn tidy men. It didn't give her much to work with. With sheer force of will, she turned herself on her back, biting back a moan against the pain. She was grateful her arms were a little numb now. She curled her legs up and swung them. Up and toward her abs, tightening them. Rolling ball. Thank god for Pilates.

And for working out four days a week and learning karate. She rolled until she had momentum and then planted her feet. It was just enough to let her roll and get to her knees.

She would love to see Derek's perfect, "never has to go to the gym because no one ever tried to kill her" sub do that. She would probably be crying prettily and waiting for her man to save her.

Derek was going to have to get used to something different.

"Leslie, where the hell are you? I thought you were right behind me and now you're not answering your phone."

As quietly as she could, she brought one foot up and then the other.

That was when she saw the lights. Red and blue and coming ever closer. He didn't have the sirens on, but he had to run the lights at the speed he was moving.

Derek was almost here.

"What the fuck?" Terry turned to the window.

Karina took her shot. She couldn't take the chance that he would off her before he ran. She brought her head forward and full-on head-butted the fucker. She practically saw stars but managed to stay on her feet.

Terry groaned and his hand went to his head. Karina saw those lights stop in front. She had to make it to the door. She couldn't run, but she was determined. She shuffled as fast as she could.

She felt a hand on her shoulder. "No, you don't, bitch."

Without a thought, she brought her head back. He'd left her with one weapon and she could use it until her skull broke. She made contact and his hand fell away.

"Fuck!"

"Derek! Derek!" He might not know what room she was in. The house seemed small but she wanted him to know exactly where to find her.

She was tackled from behind and went down hard.

"Not on your life. I'm getting out of here. Maybe they'll be too busy trying to save you to come after me." He pulled a knife out.

Karina twisted again, turning and knocking into a floor lamp that rattled and fell. She pushed back, her heels moving her along the hardwood floor.

Terry snarled and was just about to the bring the knife down when a gorgeous little red dot appeared in the middle of his chest.

The SWAT guys were going to get a show from her.

"I wouldn't move. They really like to shoot people."

The door burst open and she heard the dulcet sounds of her lover screaming for Terry to stand down.

"Drop the knife or give me one good excuse, asshole." She couldn't see him, but she heard his feet moving across the floor.

Now that her Dom was here, she was more than willing to let him handle things. His gorgeous face came into view. She heard the knife thud against the floor.

"Are you all right?" She heard other officers rushing in and then Derek knelt down beside her. His hands went to her forehead. She winced as he touched a spot on her head. "We're going to need a bus."

That was the last thing she wanted to do. She didn't want an ambulance. She wanted him to take her home, not get put through a slew of invasive medical tests she didn't need. "I don't need to go to the hospital."

His mouth firmed stubbornly as he started undoing the ropes.

"You're going."

"Hey, this was all consensual, officer." Terry had put his hands up. "My girl here is into some heavy bondage. We just came to a friend's house to play a little."

The detective who had followed Derek in was already pulling Terry's hands behind his back and slipping the cuffs on him.

Derek's eyes narrowed. "You should be very happy I don't shoot your balls off here and now."

The arresting officer had Terry firmly in hand. Fisher, if she recalled. He was a young detective under Derek's command. They had moved fast. "If you want, I can always turn my back. You know the SWAT guys love a good castration." He started to pull Terry along. "I don't think anyone's buying what you're selling, buddy. Do you want to make this official, Lieutenant?"

Derek shook his head. "I want to take care of her. You handle the trash, Fisher."

"I would take care of her, too." Fisher winked her way. "You're looking good, Mills. What the fuck was this idiot thinking coming after you? No one takes Karina out. Moron."

"Eyes to yourself, man. She's the victim, damn it. Get me something for her to wear. And you read him his Miranda rights." Derek started untangling the ropes, but he wasn't looking at her. He was studying the pattern, figuring out the fastest way to get her out, looking anywhere but her eyes.

"Derek?"

"I'll have you out in a minute and you are going to the hospital. Take a deep breath. When the feeling starts to come back, this is going to hurt." His words were tight as though he was forcing himself to speak.

"I've brought some clothes for our lovely piece of bait." Liam smiled down at her, dropping a bag on the floor. "One of the female officers had her gym clothes in her squad car. I knew you'd make it, darlin'. Damn. What did you do to your head? Did you head butt the fucker? Nice move."

Derek frowned at Li. "Could you go and wait for the ambulance? And make sure my people know she's not talking tonight. They can take statements in the morning. Fisher and I both saw him trying to kill her. With that and Starr's statement, we'll be able to hold him no problem, but she doesn't need to go anywhere but the hospital and home for tonight."

He was being a little dramatic. Yes, it had been traumatic and she'd been scared, but she could handle it. Her job alone had taught her to be cool under pressure. He should know that. "Derek, I'm fine. I have a bump on my head and my arms hurt like hell, but I can certainly talk. Where's Daley?"

She wouldn't call him Master Will where anyone could hear. That was not for vanilla ears. He'd done nothing wrong except get caught in her drama. She would try to mitigate the damage for him in any way she could.

Derek helped her sit up as he unwrapped her breasts. Terry must have studied up because he'd done a fairly decent job of imitating Shibari. "He's on his way to the hospital, too. He seems to have put up a hell of a fight before they took him down. I have no idea what they gave him. Something worse than you."

"I think it was a sedative they gave me. The way Terry talked they gave Will some drugs. They wanted them in his system when you found us here." She managed to not scream as the blood rushed back into her arms.

Derek noticed anyway. "Fucker. If he damaged nerves, I'll kill him."

He wouldn't because he was one of the good guys, but he seemed to regret it at this point. "Won't you please hold me?"

He stopped. "Karina..."

Her heart dropped. The case was over. He didn't want anyone to see him touching her in anything but a helpful capacity. It was over.

She hadn't expected that. She'd told herself she had, but she hadn't. Somewhere in the back of her head, she'd thought that he would come around. He would see that she was right for him.

He didn't.

She could hear a siren now. The ambulance.

More cops walked in, including the Rangers, and suddenly there was no more private talk. She was hauled up and given time to change. She found herself in Will Daley's rather opulent bathroom.

Karina stared at herself in the mirror. She could see the marks on her face and rope burns on her body.

But the hole in her damn heart hurt far worse.

# Chapter Twelve

"Is there anything I can do for you?" Avery sat down on the bed and reached for her hand.

Karina shook her head. "You should be at home with Aidan."

Her son was only weeks old. Karina had no idea why Liam had called her. She was fine. After numerous scans and a horrific amount of blood work, the doctor had even said she was fine. She was going to be released as soon as the paperwork was done.

To go home to her empty place. She wondered if Derek had already had someone go and pick up his things or if he would offer her a ride home. Perhaps that was why there were so many of her friends up here. Li had probably called in the troops because he knew how hard this would be on her. She had no doubt she could lie about her feelings for Brighton, but it wouldn't do her any good. Li probably knew.

That was just one more embarrassment to face.

Avery squeezed her hand. "Aidan is fine. He's happily asleep at Ashley's. I've been told that Jill and Ryan are babysitting as much as they can trying to figure out if they're ready."

The door opened and Ashley Paxon, soon-to-be Langston, walked in carrying a tray of what smelled like coffee. "Ryan won't admit it but he's scared of poop. Jill is trying to get him used to the quick change. If you don't get in there fast, my baby girl will get it everywhere."

Avery's eyes widened. "I thought we agreed to not talk about poop around the civilians."

Ashley grinned, looking even younger than twenty-five years. "Avery thinks if we lie and say it's all easy that we can trick Big Tag into giving it a go. Grace is telling him that Carys is already almost potty trained." Ashley shook her head gravely. "Yeah, so not true. As long as we keep him away from the Internet and baby info books, I think we can do it. Anytime a show with a baby comes on, Charlotte switches it over to porn. We'll get him yet."

Avery and Ashley had shown up an hour into her hospital stay with clothes and toiletries. They had sat at her side.

Derek had ridden with her in the ambulance. He'd made sure she was set up in a room and she hadn't seen him since.

When he was done, she supposed he was done.

"Well, Li shouldn't have called you. I'm fine." She would have preferred to be alone. Avery and Ashley were just reminders of how singular she was. They were both happily married and starting their lives. She wouldn't be doing that anytime soon. She hated the fact that she was thinking of her friends that way, but she'd settled into a nice little pity party.

"Li didn't call me. Derek called me. He set everything up. By the time he called me, he'd already talked to Ryan and Jill and set up babysitting. They came by and picked up Aidan on their way to Keith and Ashley's."

Ashley set a latte in front of her. "Yep, he had Keith jumping. Keith's sitting outside. He's watching the entire event like it's a soap unfolding in front of him. You should have seen Derek when the DA showed up. I thought his head was going to explode. He did that really quiet yelling thing."

She'd seen him do it. Derek was at his most dangerous when he got quiet, his voice an almost arctic low. So he'd called her friends in. Why? Had he felt guilty? Did he feel guilty because she'd gotten taken or because he was leaving her?

How was she going to face him again? She could put a smile on her face and tell him she was alright, but she had no idea how she was going to watch him play with subs at Sanctum.

Now that she knew how it felt to have his hands on her, she had no idea how she would accept another Dom.

Maybe it was time to pull back a little. She could go to more meetings, maybe see a therapist and figure out a different way to handle her stress.

There was a knock on the door and Karina almost sighed with relief. The discharge nurse. Finally.

"I think Derek told you she wasn't talking tonight," Ashley said as Maia Brighton walked in.

She looked altogether too perfect in her Chanel suit and red-soled Louboutins. Even at this time of night, her hair was in a professional-looking bun her accessories flawless. Karina had to wonder if she kept a stylist on the payroll.

Maia strode in like she owned the place. "Oh, Derek is busy with the never-ending paperwork that comes with keeping a killer off the street. You know, all in a day's work. I thought I would take this time to point out a few truths of life to Ms. Mills."

Avery frowned. "I'll go get Li. He'll take care of this."

"I think I'll just haul her out by her hair. I can do it, Karina. I've been going to the gym and she's a little skeletal." Ashley eyed the blonde like she was about to get her warrior princess on.

Maia smiled brightly. "Thank you. I do try to stay thin."

If she let this go it could get ugly, and the last thing she needed was to embarrass herself by having Brighton come in to rescue her. She could handle a little mean girl all on her own. "Guys, why don't you give us a minute? Don't bring the men into it, please."

Avery and Ashley stood and walked warily out the door.

"All right, give it your best shot," Karina said, sitting up. "I've had a shitty day so you piling on is just the topper."

"Touchy." Maia sat her bag down. Karina was sure it was a designer thing that cost more than she made in a month. Maia sighed and stared at her. "I don't like you."

The feeling was mutual. "I don't care."

Maia shrugged. "I wouldn't either. I do like Derek."

"Then you probably shouldn't have fucked around on him. Did you have to sleep with his brother?"

She thought about that for a moment before speaking again, her voice taking on a softer tone. "I did that for different reasons than he thinks. He was gone for so long. I really did miss him. His brother looks a lot like him. It doesn't matter now because I certainly can't excuse the others. I guess we are who we are. We really can't change that, can we?"

Oh, now she knew what was coming. Someone had looked up her records. Like Li had told her, sealed records didn't always stay sealed. "Are you here to blackmail me?"

Maia laughed. "Oh, honey, you don't have anything I need. At least not anything that's yours to give. You are shockingly touchy for a former crack whore."

"I never took crack and sure as hell wasn't a whore." Maybe her night wasn't done. She could take all her newfound spare time and dedicate her life to making Maia's hell. It could be her new hobby.

"The words just go well together, don't you think? Crack and whore. It's like chocolate and peanut butter."

"Yes, a little like the words beat and your ass." Her arms still ached, but she was pretty sure she could handle Maia.

Maia laughed again, this time a much purer sound. When she smiled at Karina this time, she could almost believe it was true. "All right. I do like you. But I don't want to."

"Do you want to explain to me why you're here? Derek told me I couldn't give a statement until tomorrow."

"I bet he did." Her face turned as serious as the Botox allowed. "I'm here because I've had a couple of really shitty days and it's made me think. I love Derek. I want him to be happy and he's fucking it up again."

"Ah, so you think he can't find happiness with the crack whore. Nice. Here's the good news for you. We were only supposed to play while we were working, and we are no longer working."

Maia pointed her way. "See. He's fucking up. You're fucking up. I am guilty of many, many crimes against humanity, but surprisingly enough, hypocrisy isn't one of them. I read your files. You made some mistakes. Given your youth, they're certainly understandable. If I'd grown up the way you did, I would have done as many drugs as I could have, too. The remarkable thing is that you're alive and you seem to be some sort of PI saint."

"What's your point?"

"My point is if I have to really let him go, I think you'll take care of him. You love him, right?"

"It doesn't matter how I feel. He doesn't love me."

She rolled her blue eyes. "Somehow I thought you'd fight harder."

"I made a deal with him. Look, I don't want him to stay with me because he feels bad. I do love him. I want him to have what he wants."

Maia took a moment, seeming to think about what she said next. "He hasn't slept with the same woman for more than a week since we got divorced. He's in love with you, but he also struggles to change his course. I knew the minute I heard you'd been taken that he was going to screw this up so I came down here. He's been out there issuing orders about you and making everyone crazy, but I would bet he hasn't hugged you yet."

Karina shook her head. "No."

"And you're in here ready to throw in the towel. It means nothing. It means that he went into cop mode and he's going to struggle to get out of it. Don't let him keep you away. He'll try to sleep on the couch. Maybe he's already doing that because…"

Karina held a hand up. "We fixed that shit really fast. When he has a bad dream, I set him on his ass. He's only done it twice. He does it again and I'll handle it."

Maia proved the devil could cry. A single tear fell on her cheek. "He's sleeping with you." She took a long breath. "That's good. That's really good. So when he tells you he should sleep on the couch tonight, you should…"

A deep well of sympathy flowed through Karina. No matter what a bitch Maia could be, she was trying to do something good. "I'll tell him to get his ass in our bed."

"He needs to be needed, you know. He needs to be good."

Karina nodded. "I know." It was weird, but now they had a connection. They loved the same man. "He doesn't know about my misspent youth."

Maia reached down and grabbed her purse. "So tell him."

"It's not that easy."

She huffed a little. "Really? You don't think he's going to be sympathetic to the woman who pulled herself out of hell and managed to make the people around her happy?"

"I guess I didn't think of it that way."

"Then start, sister, because he needs a woman and not a guilt-plagued martyr. You did good, Mills. You did good and you won the prize, if you play your cards right. Just make him happy and I won't have to come after you and make your life a living hell."

The door suddenly opened and Derek's big form was silhouetted against the light. "What the hell are you doing in here? I told you to leave her alone."

Maia seemed to change from slightly warm to chilly in a heartbeat. Her shoulders straightened, her spine becoming perfectly erect. "Well, she's a horrible witness. I hope the forensics are good on this one. I would hate to put her on the stand. Good-bye, Derek. I'll talk to you Monday."

"Maia," Karina called out.

Maia turned, her face a mask of indifference. "What?"

"I'll make sure you get your car back." Karma had worked. It was time for it to let up a little.

Maia's eyes widened. "You bitch. Damn it. I don't want to like you."

She turned and walked out the door.

"What was that about?" Derek strode in, looking ridiculously gorgeous and slightly distant.

How hard had it been on him? He'd had to distance himself. To think like a cop and not a lover. Sometimes it was hard for cops to come back down. It was hard for them to get back to being lovers and husbands and sons. They needed an anchor. They needed one the same way an addict needed to know someone gave a shit.

She'd been very selfish in thinking that she was the only one who needed.

"She just had a couple of questions." What had Maia said? Derek needed to be needed. It was an intrinsic part of who he was. It was why he'd sought out the lifestyle. It was why he'd become a Dom. Karina had been on her own for a very long time, but she remembered how it felt to rely on someone. "Sir, I'm very tired. Could you take me home?"

He stopped, obviously startled, and then he jumped into action like an eager puppy. "I'll get the nurse."

He practically ran out of the room.

He wasn't trying to get rid of her. He was just a man who struggled to shift gears and it was her damn job to help him.

It was also her job to trust him.

If she loved him, she would risk losing him, but suddenly she thought she would take that bet. She had been strong. She had pulled herself out.

And sometimes, just sometimes, the universe rewarded a girl for that.

\* \* \* \*

Derek held the door open for her. His house. He'd given her a cock-and-bull story about hiding out from the press, but the truth was he wanted her in his space for once. He'd been out of control all night, with her in danger. He wanted to fucking control things for once.

She was so pale as she walked toward him. He had to remember that she'd been through hell. She'd been taken right out from under his nose. She had to have been terrified. She had to be pissed at him for letting it happen. Her arms had to ache. The fucker had tied her far too tight. What the hell had he been thinking?

*He'd been thinking about killing her. She'd almost fucking died. She had to fight for her damn life, you idiot. So back the fuck off and give her space.*

He would take the spare bedroom. The bed there sucked, but she needed rest and he needed to know that she was comfortable. He needed her to be happy here because he was going to try to make sure she never left.

How the fuck did he do that? How did he get her to forgive him for putting her in danger? His heart was still pumping, his adrenaline not anywhere close to normal.

What if he'd done something wrong? What if he forgot some tiny legality that meant Terry Mills went free?

Karina stopped in front of him, bringing her hand to caress his face. Damn, but everywhere she touched him turned soft and warm. Except his fucking cock. "Are you okay?"

Naturally she would ask that. She was that kind of woman. "I'm fine. Are you hungry?"

She gave him a slight smile. "No. Avery and Ashley stuffed me with snacks."

He'd made sure her friends showed up. He hadn't been able to get hold of Serena, and Grace was dealing with a sick baby, but he'd gotten Avery and Ashley to the hospital. She needed her friends. She needed to know she was loved.

She'd been through something horrible. She should be surrounded by love. He just wasn't sure she wanted his.

Karina strode through the door. She had only a small bag. Avery and Liam had gone by her place and picked up some clothes and essentials for her. She carried them in now. "Where's the bedroom?"

He pointed to the master. He wouldn't give her anything but the best. She would be secure there. He would watch over her for as long as she let him. "Right back there."

She sighed and walked toward the room. She stopped at the doorway. "Are you coming?"

"Uhm, I'll get you something to drink." He wouldn't be coming for a long time. It might take a while for her to recover and then he needed to make sure she was ready. He needed to make her understand he was serious about this relationship and that he wouldn't accept just being her boyfriend.

Had he earned that? Had he truly earned being her Master and husband?

He sounded like a fucking idiot. He was going to get her a drink? A drink for a woman who never drank?

It was a thing he added to his list of ever growing crap he needed to fix about his life, all of it concerning Karina.

She walked through the doorway, leaving it open. Damn but she should have closed it because he could sort of see her. He watched as she put her bag on the bed and then shrugged off her clothes. Her perfect skin came into view. She was naturally tan due to her DNA. He would bet she wasn't entirely Caucasian. Her skin was rich and had a glorious olive tone. His exotic girl. A harem of one because he didn't need anyone but her.

He was a jerk. He shouldn't be thinking of her that way. She'd been stripped down and hurt. She didn't need another man thinking about using her.

He would take his time. He would let her know that he was here for her. He would handle the case and then she would know he cared.

Yeah. His dick hated him.

She walked through the doorway and his eyes went wicked wide. "Karina?"

She was standing there completely nude. Her full breasts were pointed out, the nipples so sweetly puckered his dick couldn't help but respond. She gave him a "goddess of the earth and sea and sex" smile as she stared his way. "Hey, baby. Can you come to bed now?"

His cock damn near jumped off his body and ran to her, but he owed her more. "You need to rest."

Her smile dimmed. She was still naked, but she looked vulnerable. He still thought it was so fucking sexy. "My mom died when I was five."

He went utterly still. "Really?"

"Yes." Her face had flushed. Her whole body really. She stepped into the living room, her body moving with the grace of a person who didn't care that she was undressed. She lowered herself on his couch gingerly, sitting on the edge. "I was just a kid. I didn't find her. I came home from school and the social services woman was there. She was a good mom but she liked to get high. She did a lot for her drugs."

She did not need to do this tonight. "Bab...Karina, go to bed. It's okay. We can talk in the morning. Or not."

Her lips curled to the sweetest smile. "Because you don't care?"

That wasn't the truth. "I care. I care a lot. I just...Karina, you're crying."

He'd fucked up again. She'd been through hell and only now was she crying. He'd been the one to bring her low.

"I'm worried that you won't love me when I tell you my story, and I love you so much I think I'll die if you can't love me back."

His heart skipped a beat. "What?"

She turned to him and patted the seat beside her. "I said I love you. Please listen to me and then you can tell me if you think you might be able to love me back."

He loved her. He loved her with every fiber of his being. The story she was about to tell him wouldn't change that in the slightest. He didn't care. He loved the Karina who sat in front of him, the Karina who—if he had any say in it—would bear his children and hold his hand when they were old and gray. He loved the Karina who was strong and beautiful and who could save herself.

But this was her story to tell and he was going to listen.

She seemed to take his silence as acquiescence. "I have no idea who my dad is. He could be alive or dead. I don't know. I went into foster care. I was okay for a long time. I got adopted. Her name was Marcy Giles and she was so nice. I was fourteen when she died. Car accident this time. I had a sister by then. Regina. She was two years older than me and I tried so hard to keep us together. There was no blood between us. Regina was born with Downs. Marcy didn't care. I didn't care. The state did. She died when I was sixteen. I only found out because I ran away to her halfway house."

So much death for someone so young. He couldn't stop himself. She was naked and offering herself to him. Not in a sexual way. She was giving him her pain so he could understand her. So he could take a piece of it into himself and make it less of a burden on her heart. He reached for her because this story was best told when she was in his arms, safe, loved.

He would take all of her pain and halve it because she belonged to him. Her pain, her soul, was a beautiful half of his. "I'm sorry to hear that. What happened to you?"

She sank into him, her shoulder finding his neck. Trusting. Her arms wound around him. No hesitation. She was his. "I got shuffled around. Some of my foster parents were good. Some weren't so good. A couple...they used their position against me."

He tightened his arms around her. She'd been abused. He wanted to go back and protect her but all he could really do was love the woman she was, to worship her for her beauty, her survival. There was something so strong, so vivid about the woman she was now. "I love you."

Her head turned up. "Don't say that yet."

He already knew what she was going to say. He'd figured it out long ago. Emotion welled inside him. "I will love you until I can't breathe anymore. And long after. I believe, Karina. I believe there is a heaven and if I go first, I will wait for you. Don't say you can't go there. God is greater than we make him. Bigger than we think he is."

"I did drugs. A lot of them."

So many people would have. "It doesn't matter."

His faith could take them far past where her legacy could. She'd been dealt a bad card. He had a full deck and he would share it with her.

"Derek, I did hard stuff."

A deep peace settled over him. She trusted him. She was talking to him. Now he had to make her believe because they had a shot—a shot at life together, a shot at love, and that was all either of them could ask for. There were no guarantees. She could die tomorrow. She could change. She could fall away from him.

So many things could go wrong but he needed one thing, just one thing to go right. "I love you."

"I was arrested twice and the only reason I don't have an adult record is because Kevin sent me to rehab."

She thought she could turn him away? He was made of stronger stuff than that. It was time to turn his back on his marriage. That had been crap but he'd seen real love. He saw it when his father looked at his mother. And he fucking saw it in the mirror because he was in love with her and that wouldn't stop. It was a terminal condition. He would love her forever. "It doesn't matter because I love you."

"Derek, you don't understand. It was bad. My rehab was awful. I couldn't keep anything down for days. I wanted to die."

"I'm glad you didn't because I love you." There was only one truth and he was going to make her believe.

"When Kevin found me I was living in a house where they cooked meth and ran drugs, and I was two steps away from selling my body because I didn't care. The drugs were all that mattered."

He pulled her into his lap, wrapping his arms around her. She was his love. So brave. So smart. "I love you."

Slowly, so slowly, her arms wrapped around him and they were together in a way they had never been before. Halves of a whole. He was the boy who had everything and still felt hollow and she was the girl with nothing who had so much to give.

Together they were complete.

She started talking. She told him about how alone she'd felt, how she'd been kicked to the curb at seventeen and found herself in a meth house. She'd had nowhere to go, but somehow she'd helped the people around her. She talked about the deal she'd made with Kevin. It sounded easy, but he knew damn well how much strength it had taken.

She'd conquered something so few people ever did. She'd faced it and come out stronger. Her words made him think she thought less of herself because she needed to go to meetings and talk, but he was in awe of her resilience.

Karina fell silent, her head against his chest. After a long moment, she spoke in hesitating tones. "Derck, I understand if you need to think about it."

"Marry me." He didn't need to think about it. He loved her. He needed her to react emotionally before she really thought about the fact that he didn't deserve her. He would worship the ground she walked on, would feel blessed for every day he lived with her.

"Derek? Did you hear a word I said?"

Brat. Little fucking brat. Did she think he'd drifted and decided that the only way he could appease her was to ask her to marry him? She'd walked out naked. She'd meant something by that. She'd offered her submission by offering her body. "Knees, Karina."

She slid off his lap, getting to her knees in front of him. He touched her hair and forced her to look at him.

"Karina, listen to me and listen well. I love you. I want you to marry me. I want you to call me husband in front of the world and Master in our safe places. I want you to trust that I will always take care of you."

"I love you, Derek. Master. I love you but for a long time that felt wrong because I loved him, too."

"I'm not asking you to forget about him. Tell me your stories, but, baby you have to let me be a part of them." It was so hard to remember. "I'm sorry."

She shook her head. "No, baby. I'm sorry. He called me that and I felt guilty because I wanted you to call me that more than anything. I loved Kevin. I did. But I've never wanted a man the way I want you."

"That's good because god knows I want you." His cock pulsed and there was no way he left her alone for the night. "How much do your arms hurt, baby?"

Her lips curled into a sexy grin. "I don't think you'll be tying me up for a few weeks, but I can handle whatever else you want to throw at me, Master."

"I'm glad you said that because I'm dying here. Help me out."

Her hands went to the fly of his jeans. She made quick work of the button, releasing his cock. Her hand went around him, holding him in a tight grip. His girl wasn't tentative. She knew what he liked and she gave it to him. He liked her rough, strong, giving as much as she took.

Yeah, he'd been an idiot and he'd wasted so much time, but he wasn't going to waste another second. She stroked him, her eyes on his dick as she licked her lips. That made him feel about twelve feet tall. "You're going to marry me, baby."

"Yes I am," she replied. "I'm going to marry you because I love you and you keep a really clean house."

Brat. "I would spank you if you hadn't already been through hell."

Her eyes came up as she licked the head of his cock. "I think you can come up with a way to make me feel better. I know I can make you forget about our crappy night."

If he let her, she'd suck him dry and while that was usually a damn fine idea, he had other plans for tonight. It was his turn to be the supplicant. He gripped her wrist gently and pulled it away. He didn't want to come until he was deep inside her. "Karina, I don't want to wear a condom. I don't want to wait."

All of their friends were having kids. There would be a big group of them running crazy and wild and growing up together. He wanted that for his kids. His and Karina's. Damn but her daughter would be a handful.

A brilliant smile crossed her face. "I'm not getting any younger, Master. I think I would like to be a mom very much."

She moved back and let him stand. He quickly got out of his jeans and boots and shrugged off his shirt. He held a hand out to help her stand, but the minute she got to her feet, he leaned down and gently picked her up.

Her arm went around his neck and a dreamy look crossed her face. "I love it when you do that, Brighton. Somehow you make me feel dainty."

She was dainty compared to him. He started for his bedroom. Finally, finally she would be where she belonged. In his bed. "Then I'll just carry you everywhere."

She laughed. "I think that might make it hard for me to work."

Another thing to talk about. "Baby, I know you love what you do, but can you tone down the dangerous stuff? Please. You're going to give me a heart attack."

"I can't have that." She touched his jaw, brushing her fingers against the bristles there. "I think I'm going to take some time off and see if I can put that money Terry was willing to kill me over to good use. I've hidden so much of myself for a long time. I'm ready to talk, Derek. I'm ready to stand up. I think DPD can help me with a youth outreach."

Oh, shit. She was going to be the bossiest community advocate any of them had ever worked with, and he would love every minute of sparring with her. "I can make that happen."

Because making sure she got what she needed was his job.

When she gave him hell, he would just have to take her to the bedroom where he could be the boss.

He laid her down on his bed, turning on the light on the nightstand. He was damn glad he'd never had a woman here. He'd always gone to the woman's place, telling himself this was his space, but now he realized the truth. Somewhere deep down, he'd been waiting for her.

He stared at her, memorizing the vision of her golden skin laid out, her face open and trusting. This, this was the start of his life, and he didn't want to forget a second of it.

"Derek?" Karina held her hand out.

He took it, joining her on the bed. He touched the place on her forehead where a lump had formed. She'd fought like hell.

"Don't think about it, Derek. It's just a little bump. It doesn't even hurt. It won't scar."

He kissed that little lump that she'd gotten while fighting for her life. And then he kissed the small scar on her cheek that wasn't even noticeable under makeup. "Your scars are beautiful."

He kissed them all, finding even the smallest of places where she'd once been hurt and lavishing affection there.

She protested and giggled when he flipped her over and caressed every inch of her skin. "You're making me crazy. Kiss me."

"I am kissing you and this is my time, so you be still." It was his time to explore her body with no limits, no walls between them. He kissed the nape of her neck, nibbled on her earlobes, and licked his way down her spine. He kissed everywhere those damn ropes had burned. His ropes were the only ones that would ever touch her again. He would bind her in silk and make her feel his love, his devotion.

He could smell her arousal. He chuckled a little as he noticed her hands were fisted in the bedspread.

"Do you want something, baby?" He loved making her beg.

"You know what I want. So give it to me."

Oh, she really was asking for it. He gave her ass a quick but hard smack. "That was your warning. I'm not going to give you a full-on spanking no matter how much you beg. You might think you know best, but I'm in charge here. I will continue to play with you and not allow you to come."

She whimpered a little, the sound making his cock jump. "Please, Master."

"That's better." He kissed the place he'd just spanked. "Now ask me for what you want. Use words that get me hot and ready for you."

He loved it when she talked dirty.

"I want your cock, Master. Please give me your cock."

He turned her over, loving the way her skin had flushed. He let his fingers find her pussy. Wet. Soft. His. His fingers parted her labia as she whimpered again and closed her eyes, giving over to him. He played for a minute, fucking her with a single finger while his thumb found her clit.

"Is that not enough, baby?"

She shook her head. "You know it's not enough. I need your cock."

But she would take what he gave her and he wanted more than whimpering cries. He wanted to make her scream because he wasn't sure how long he would last once he got inside her. There was too much emotion riding him, too much longing.

He gave her a second finger, curling them inside her to find her sweet spot. He leaned over and sucked her clit.

She screamed his name as she came.

And then he was done with waiting. He covered her body with his and was finally where he'd needed to be all night. Skin to skin. His chest to hers, their legs tangled, their eyes meeting. He made a place for himself between her legs and smoothed her hair back. "I love you."

"I love you, too." Her arms wound around him, binding him as securely as he bound her with ropes. She didn't need ropes. She just needed to be close to him to make him feel safe.

He leaned down and kissed her, thrusting his tongue in even as his cock found its home. He pushed deep inside her in a single ruthless thrust. She groaned against his mouth.

She pulsed around him, her pussy tight as a vise. So hot. So fucking good.

Over and over he thrust inside, keeping his body tight to hers, wanting nothing at all between them.

Her legs wound around him and he was utterly enveloped in her.

She kept pace with him, matching him thrust for thrust and leaving her mark on his back. He loved the way she fought for her pleasure, gave him everything she had.

But it was too sweet to last. He felt his spine tingle, his balls drawing up and ready to blow. Anticipation flashed through him. This wasn't the end, just the beginning. He would make love to his wife for the rest of his life.

He ground down against her clit as he thrust in as far as he could go.

Karina tightened around him, holding on as she moaned and rode the wave of her orgasm. She clung to him as pure pleasure swamped his system. He lost his rigid control and plunged mindlessly into her. Over and over he thrust, giving her everything he had, giving up every ounce of come.

He finally couldn't move again and let his body fall to hers. Her hands found his hair, sinking in and holding him to her body.

He let his head rest against her breast and promised to never let her go again.

# Epilogue

Karina dropped her Styrofoam cup in the trash. All around her the meeting was breaking up. Some of the members were old friends and some came and went, their faces fleeting in her memory. They were all passengers on a journey they took together, a journey they chose to take because they'd decided life was worth more than a momentary high. So much more.

"I heard a rumor that you're going to be doing some charity work," the meeting leader said with a grin. Howard had been running the three p.m. every day for years.

"As soon as I can find a space." She was beyond excited about this new chapter in her life. She was in the planning stages, but she was going to start a youth outreach that helped young drug offenders find rehab instead of jail, an education instead of death. "And I've been told by my soon-to-be mother-in-law that everything can wait until after the wedding."

She'd never imagined it, but she was having a big church wedding complete with a white dress and all the trappings. Derek had gone a little pale at the thought and started to argue that they could just elope, but Karina knew a woman on a mission when she saw one.

"Congratulations to you. You're looking good for a woman who nearly died."

She let out a rueful laugh. It had made the news and several papers. "I'm good. Terry's trial is coming up but I'm not really worried that he'll get off. The prosecutor is a shark."

And had sort of weirdly become a friend. Maia had promised both her and Derek that Terry would spend the rest of his life in prison. Of course, she'd actually said he'd spend the rest of his life being someone's chew toy, but that was just how she talked. Maia seemed perfectly happy prosecuting a case she was sure would get her plenty of TV time.

Then there was Will, who just seemed to want everything to go away. She'd been trying to talk to him, trying to get him to come to Sanctum, but so far he'd ducked all her calls. She had to hope he wouldn't ignore his needs for too long.

"I'm glad to hear that." Howard patted her shoulder.

"Thanks. I'll see you next time."

He gave her a grin. "I bet you will. And bring the grim reaper with you. We're getting used to him."

Derek wouldn't let her come alone. If she needed to go, he would drop what he was doing and drive her and sit outside the church until she walked out. He would be there, waiting to hold her hand.

She stepped outside feeling lighter than she had in forever.

Derek looked over at her and smiled.

Damn, but she felt young again. Two weeks of being engaged to Derek and she seemed to have lost twenty years' worth of guilt. The minute that man looked at her, she felt young and clean and free.

"Are you ready, baby?" He held his hand out.

She took it. "Yes."

She was ready. Ready for her third life because sometimes, if a girl was really lucky, sometimes, she got a third chance.

Karina was ready to take it.

Sign up for the 1001 Dark Nights Newsletter
and be entered to win a Tiffany Key necklace.
There's a contest every month!

Visit www.1001DarkNights.com/key/to subscribe.

As a bonus, all newsletter subscribers will receive a free
1001 Dark Nights story:

*The First Night*
by Shayla Black, Lexi Blake & M.J. Rose

Turn the page for a full list of the
1001 Dark Nights fabulous novellas...

# 1001 Dark Nights

FOREVER WICKED
A Wicked Lovers Novella
by Shayla Black

CRIMSON TWILIGHT
A Krewe of Hunters Novella
by Heather Graham

CAPTURED IN SURRENDER
A MacKenzie Family Novella
by Liliana Hart

SILENT BITE: A SCANGUARDS WEDDING
A Scanguards Vampire Novella
by Tina Folsom

DUNGEON GAMES
A Masters and Mercenaries Novella
by Lexi Blake

AZAGOTH
A Demonica Novella
by Larissa Ione

NEED YOU NOW
by Lisa Renee Jones

SHOW ME, BABY
A Masters of the Shadowlands Novella
by Cherise Sinclair

ROPED IN
A Blacktop Cowboys ® Novella
by Lorelei James

TEMPTED BY MIDNIGHT
A Midnight Breed Novella
by Lara Adrian

THE FLAME
by Christopher Rice

CARESS OF DARKNESS
A Phoenix Brotherhood Novella
by Julie Kenner


*Also from Evil Eye Concepts:*
TAME ME
A Stark International Novella
by J. Kenner

# Acknowledgements from the Author

I want to send out a huge thank you to Liz Berry and MJ Rose and the entire crew at Evil Eye Concepts. I think you're changing the world of publishing and I'm so happy you chose to take me along for the ride.

Lots of love to the October Girls – you know who you are. May we have many years of shots and pool time and crazy men who throw towels and jello shots at us from the balcony!

As always thanks to my crew – Rich, Chloe, Riane, and Stormy. I couldn't do it without you!

# About Lexi Blake

Lexi Blake lives in North Texas with her husband, three kids, and the laziest rescue dog in the world. She began writing at a young age, concentrating on plays and journalism. It wasn't until she started writing romance that she found success. She likes to find humor in the strangest places. Lexi believes in happy endings no matter how odd the couple, threesome or foursome may seem. She also writes contemporary Western ménage as Sophie Oak.

Connect with Lexi online:

Facebook: Lexi Blake
Twitter: https://twitter.com/authorlexiblake
Website: www.LexiBlake.net

Sign up for Lexi's free newsletter at www.lexiblake.net/contact.

# A View to a Thrill

Master and Mercenaries, Book 7
By Lexi Blake
Coming August 19, 2014

*A Spy without a Country*

Simon Weston grew up royal in a place where aristocracy still mattered. Serving Queen and country meant everything to him, until MI6 marked him as damaged goods and he left his home in disgrace. Ian Taggart showed him a better way to serve his fellow man and introduced him to Sanctum, a place to pursue his passion for Dominance and submission. Topping beautiful subs was a lovely distraction until he met Chelsea, and becoming her Master turned into Simon's most important mission.

*A Woman without Hope*

Chelsea Dennis grew up a pawn to the Russian mob. Her father's violent lessons taught her that monsters lurked inside every man and they should never be trusted. Hiding in the shadows, she became something that even the monsters would fear—an information broker who exposed their dirty secrets and toppled their empires. Everything changed when Simon Weston crossed her path. Valiant and faithful, he was everything she needed—and a risk she couldn't afford to take.

*A Force too Strong to Resist*

When dark forces from her past threaten her newfound family at Sanctum, Chelsea must turn to Simon, the one man she can trust with her darkest secrets. Their only chance to survive lies in a mystery even Chelsea has been unable to solve. As they race to uncover the truth and stay one step ahead of the assassins on their heels, they will discover a love too powerful to deny. But to stop a killer, Simon just might have to sacrifice himself…

\* \* \* \*

Chelsea looked at the bed that dominated the room. The only bed. Somehow she'd managed to find the shitty motel that didn't have two queens. No. It was way worse. It was a single queen and there was no couch. And she was pretty sure the floor was covered in disease. "I think I should sleep somewhere else. We need to find another room."

Blue eyes stared a hole through her. Somehow his eyes managed to be cold and hot given his mood. The color shifted, lighter, icier when he was angry. As warm as the Caribbean when he was happy.

They often seemed so cold when he looked at her. "Your contact said to meet here. We're staying here."

"He told me to meet him here. I'm sure they have another room, Weston. You don't have to sit up all night." Because there was no way they could share that bed. It was too small. He would take up all the space.

He locked the door and set down his duffel bag on the table. He shrugged out of his jacket because the man wore a three-piece suit on the run. She couldn't help but stare at his broad shoulders and the way his dress shirt tapered down to perfectly pressed slacks. He tugged at the silver tie he was wearing, pulling it free and working the buttons at his throat until she could see the start of his truly impressive chest.

God, she hoped she wasn't drooling.

The shoulder holster was the next to go in his inadvertent striptease. "You should get settled in. We have to be up early in the morning. I'll take the side closest to the door."

He couldn't be serious. "Simon, there's not enough room on that bed."

He threw that gorgeous body down, making the springs squeak. "Of course there is, love. You Americans just like to take up an enormous amount of space. When I was a child, my brother and I slept in beds much smaller than this."

"I'm not your brother, Simon."

"I understand that fully. Believe me."

She needed to take charge or she would make a complete fool of herself. "Look, Weston, you turned down my offer."

He turned lazily, one hand coming up to balance his head. He looked like a pinup in a women's magazine—all lean and predatory lines. She could see the write-up in her head. *Simon likes tea, Scotch and eating subs for breakfast.* His turn-offs include everything that comes out of Chelsea Dennis's mouth. "Are you talking about your very charming offer to use my body to lose your virginity?"

She hadn't put it like that. "You don't want me. I get it. So let's keep things simple. I hired you. I'm the boss. I'm going to see if I can rent the room next to this one and that can be yours."

He didn't move. He didn't have to. She saw the way his eyes narrowed and then his voice came out, low and in that perfect upper-crust British accent that made her nipples hard. Her nipples were really stupid and she wished they didn't like him so damn much. "You're under a grave misapprehension, Chelsea. You are not my boss and you did not hire me. You came to me with a problem and I told you I would solve it. I believe I also mentioned that I was in charge and that was the only way I do this for you. So you will take off your clothes and you will get into this bed and you will sleep beside me tonight. I explained this to you when you signed the bloody contract. Do I need to explain what the word submissive means?"

Tears pricked her eyes. He was so damn unfair. She had to wonder if she would ever find a man who didn't want to punish her. "You forced me to sign that contract."

Now he moved, rolling to the side of the bed and getting to his feet with pure predatory grace. "I did nothing of the kind."

He seemed very willing to revise history. She wasn't about to let him forget. "If I hadn't signed your contract, you would have let me die."

He sighed, a long-suffering sound. "I certainly would not and if you think that's true then you don't know me at all. Perhaps I should do exactly what I should have done in the first place, what I would have done if you hadn't signed the contract."

That was worse than letting her die. "Please don't call Ian."

His shoulders weren't so straight as he turned and stared at her. "You're reckless, Chelsea. If I give up even a moment's control, I'll lose you and I can't stand the thought of that. The only way to save you is to be your Master and the only Master you'll accept is not the kind I want to be."

"And what kind do you want to be?"

"Indulgent. Loving. Kind. I want a sub who obeys me in the field because she understands I would never let anyone hurt her. I want the play to just be play. I want a sub who trusts me with her body, who wants me and not just some faceless Dom who'll work her over and then walk away. And I certainly don't want to be a curiosity."

She felt embarrassment flash through her system. If she could take back that first night's utter idiocy she would. She should have known he wouldn't want her. Not like that. "I get it. I got it when you turned me down the first time. I can get into bed with you because you won't touch me."

He was suddenly in her space. He'd moved so quickly she wasn't sure how he'd gotten there. One minute there was a bed between them and the next she was backing up until she hit the wall because he was stalking her. She'd gone as far as she could go, but he kept coming. He loomed over her, using every one of his six feet two inches. "I've tried to be polite about this, but you don't want that, do you? You don't want me to be a gentleman about this. You want me to take you because then you'll bloody well get it over with and you can put me in the same box with all the other men who hurt you and used you and cast you aside. I would be just one more villain who did something to you."

"I never said that."

"You don't have to. I understand you, Chelsea. You can't comprehend that, but I do. I understand you like no other man will. So I understand that I have to explain certain things to you." He moved closer until his mouth hovered above hers, his heat sinking into her skin. "I'm going to tell you how this is going to go. We'll get into that bed and I'm going to put my hands on you and I'm going to put my mouth on you. I'm going to taste you. I swear by the time you get out of that bed in the morning, you're going to know what it feels like to come against my tongue. That screaming you heard as we walked in, you're going to make that girl's orgasm sound like the squeaking of a mouse. But the one thing you won't get is my cock. You won't get that because I'm not going to take your virginity because you're curious. I'll take it when you can't think about anything but me. I'll take it when you cry out my name and tell me there's no other man you'll ever love the way you love me. Then and only then will I take what belongs to me. Am I understood?"

She managed to nod.

He took a step back and she immediately missed his heat. His hands went to the buttons on his shirt. "Then take off those bloody clothes and get in bed."

With shaking hands, she started to undress.

# Also from Lexi Blake

## EROTIC ROMANCE

*Masters And Mercenaries*
The Dom Who Loved Me
The Men With The Golden Cuffs
A Dom Is Forever
On Her Master's Secret Service
Sanctum: A Masters and Mercenaries Novella
Love and Let Die
Unconditional: A Masters and Mercenaries Novella
Dungeon Royale
Dungeon Games: A Masters and Mercenaries Novella
A View to a Thrill, *Coming August 19, 2014*

*Masters Of Ménage* (by Shayla Black and Lexi Blake)
Their Virgin Captive
Their Virgin's Secret
Their Virgin Concubine
Their Virgin Princess
Their Virgin Hostage
Their Virgin Secretary

## CONTEMPORARY WESTERN ROMANCE

*Wild Western Nights*
Leaving Camelot, Coming Soon

## URBAN FANTASY

*Thieves*
Steal the Light
Steal the Day
Steal the Moon
Steal the Sun
Steal the Night, *Coming June 2014*

# On behalf of 1001 Dark Nights,
# Liz Berry and M.J. Rose would like to thank ~

Doug Scofield
Steve Berry
Richard Blake
Dan Slater
Asha Hossain
Chris Graham
Kim Guidroz
BookTrib After Dark
Jillian Stein
and Simon Lipskar

CPSIA information can be obtained at www.ICGtesting.com
Printed in the USA
LVOW08s0151161014

408902LV00002BB/611/P